Illustration and graphic design by Jacob Hochstedler

War in October

Nicholas Hochstedler

Katie,

You are an amazing woman, organizer, and friend. I am so happy to know you!

Nicholas Hochstedler 2016

For my loving and supporting family — especially my mother, who loves crazy people, my cousin Joel, who is crazy, and my Grandpa Gaffin, who hates being told what to do.

And for all the soldiers and veterans worldwide...

I

She could explain everything else. His reclusive tendencies were his way of reclaiming his autonomy. His nightmares were replays of haunting memories. His hostility towards his medical team was the externalization of his fear. She even knew that his aggression towards her was his coping strategy for his wife's death and his choice to leave his eleven year-old daughter for war. But these "Suits", as he called them: these foreboding black suited illusions, dark hair and sunglasses, headsets in their ears, unflinching, unsmiling, faceless — standing at attention never far away from a tree or a shrub or a night-black Impala set to accelerate into an invisible getaway, *watching, watching, always watching* — how could she explain them away? He'd be in the corner of his dust-lit living room, dried old man spittle on the side of his mouth, sitting still with his feet up in his tattered green recliner, a faded quilt with frayed threads draped over his legs, silent and unmoving at the edge of the built-in foot rest and

"SHIT!"

turn towards the creamy shades, flick a small opening in two blinds with a boney finger and press his eyes to the window: *"A twig snapped in the rock garden! The Suits are doing a parameter check, the bastards!"* He'd then peer through the vinyl aperture for hours, an old man staring into nothingness.

Tonight, at about 11:13pm, Walter should have long since taken his medication and gone to bed. Instead, he was passed out in his recliner, his pills sitting dusty on the sill next to a half-drunk glass of water. She looked up at him before returning to her latest work report, burying herself in the details and growing unaware of the passing time.

The sudden creak of the worn recliner footrest folding up under the old man's nervous command followed by the sound of the metal springs grind-clicking into place behind his calves warned her to put down her reading. She looked up to catch sight of Walter launching from the rocking recliner and onto his flat feet. He threw out his crooked arms to prevent himself from falling and scurried to the door in a clumsy panic, scrambling for the porch light switch on the outdated vinyl wall. *"THE SUITS!"* he cried in ecstatic terror, *"THE SUITS!"* He tore the door open, stumbling into the yellow light of his front yard.

"There they go!"

She was already at the threshold of the door, looking

into the cold October night. Breeze rustled the leaves and flitted through the tips of buried grass, green blades starting their easy fade to brown as fall began its slow, nonchalant surrender to winter. Walter stood in the driveway underneath the moonlight, screaming.

"YOU BASTARDS! I FUCKING SEE YOU!"

Walter's words shook the night. Somewhere in the quiet neighborhood, worried lights flickered on. There was the distant sound of dogs barking. She was too tired to try.

October was always the hardest month, and the anniversary of his wife's death was this Wednesday. She sighed. It was probably one of her many obligations as a daughter to a mentally unstable war veteran to stop him from screaming obscenities into a quiet Sunday evening. Or, at the very least, make him wear more layers.

Well, she thought, *this is a man that literally showed up to volunteer in goggles and gloves and dangled a dog by the collar up over his head so he could get a good look at his butthole...*She looked down at Walter seething under the porch light, shaking his veiny fists in rage: *Those hands have been inside a dog's ass.* As exasperated as she was, she started laughing.

Walter cursed the moon.

She couldn't stop laughing.

II

They're coming for me. They know I know what I know. They know I know what they know. That ring-leadin' bitch of a daughter and those bastards, the ones with their scrubs, coming over to my goddamn home, right through the front door without wiping their shoes on the welcome mat, tracking mud onto my clean beige carpets with their "nurse" shoes because no matter how many goddamn times I tell them to TAKE THEIR FUCKING SHOES OFF WHEN THEY COME IN MY HOME they refuse to listen to a single word I say: those bastards, are coming for me.

It's funny, really.

They think I'm fucking stupid or something. They say their wardrobe is "standard" and they can't take their goddamn shoes off because they need to be "sanitary." But if you can't take your shoes off in another man's home when he asks politely, there's a problem. The problem with these "nurses" is this: they have something in their shoes they don't want a man to see. And those scrubs? Some nice, loose fitting clothing to

4

hide a microphone, or a gun, or some clean black clothes like
they wear outside my home under the trees and in their black
Impalas, throw 'em on overtop just in time to make me eat pills
and tell all my memories and fears and put me in a pity box
and set goals for me to climb out, controlling my strengths and
hopes too, even my family and my history; tell me she's still
alive and just grew up while I was away, that time's passed and
we all look different — that's why I can't remember her —
meanwhile she calls me Dad and comes over every fucking day
to ensure her legal right to snoop into the deepest corners of
my home, finding what I have, who I am — reminding me to
take my medicine and be a good little boy for the doctor so she
can control my regimen, my house, my life. And it's all because
I know what I know.

And one thing I know is my daughter's dead.

Walter's mind was racing again. His heartbeat quickened as
illusory images overtook his periphery. He spun, but the
apparitions dissolved. Sweating, he ran into his bedroom,
thrusting the oaken door shut behind him and immediately
locking the deadbolt. Collapsing upon the floor, he wondered
what was reality and what wasn't, or if that doing either was
even possible.

"Dad? Are you alright?" she asked.

I'm not going to fucking answer her. Maybe if I stay in here she'll go the fuck away. Haha. They hate it that I lock myself in here, saying I'm exhibiting classic "avoidance behavior" — yer goddamn right I am! I'm avoiding you bastards, and I'm plotting. Just like you, I'm plotting.

Walter smiled to himself, recalling their anger when he installed a high security lock on the inside of his bedroom door. Once, he locked himself in his room for 36 hours, refusing to respond to anyone or anything. He silently waited for the cries of concern to stop, and he plotted. Until the cops came.

"Dad," she pleaded, "it's me, *your daughter.*"

You're the farthest thing from my sweet daughter. You're the leader of this gang of goddamn criminal mastermindin' pieces of shit — sure, you all play along, you ask questions and the doctors and nurses all humor me, and they say some shit like "family support is the most important thing" and "make sure to stick to his regimen" or or or "remind him to take his medicine at 8am and 8pm" and a'course "don't overstimulate him" and "I got my goddamn head up my ass!" — these motherfuckers! I know the game. She tells me where to be and when. And I know just's well as anybody that if you control a man's space and time then you control his whole goddamn life: he's a goner, cause hell, there ain't nothin' for him to do in space and time but make the few choices he can make with what he got. And what I got is a regimented life inside a prison-style home with a gang of pricks watching my every move — so you know my time and space — and it ain't like I got too many fucking decisions to make on my own. She sees to that. She's always here — I'm never alone so I'm never free.

But I gotta closet fulla cheap beer in my bedroom you don't know about, and you can't watch me all the time. And when you ain't watchin', I—

"Dad, please relax."

The words brought Walter from the recesses of his mind to the cold sharpness of reality. He struggled to distinguish the real from the surreal often, but right now, reality was his nostrils filled with the faint scent of old carpet and the dim outline of his bedroom door, the hallway light spilling gently underneath the frame, left side of his face digging into the short bristles of carpet softly burning his ear. He could imagine her standing outside the door: right hand against her rose-soft cheek, left hand folded across her body to cup her elbow, a concerned look on her gentle face. He could envision the slow tear form in her right eye, just below the blue-gray iris, rolling down, down, down her soft cheek like a melancholy whisper, gravity pulling it off her beautiful face and sending it free falling to the beige hallway carpet. His left ear felt the soft thud of the tear hit the hallway floor. His left eye barely made out the impact of the tear and its heavy head folding in on itself, only to expand back out again into a short lazy flood halfway absorbed by the carpet. As he waited for the "pat" of the second tear, he gazed through the old oak door — right through the varnish and woodworked cuts, past the lattices of golden brown splinters, into the hallway. There she stood, the second tear welling in her right eye, a small sad pool slowly growing in her left. She sighed and let her head fall ever so slightly, a few strands of her glowing brown hair shielding her eyes, the rest tied back modestly in a shining brunette ponytail. He waited for the soft thud of the second tear. By then, it would all be over.

She's just like my wife.

Walter's heart pounded, quick and painful. He could feel the silence pour around him, immuring his body, slowly darkening his periphery and flooding his ears like black sand in a bedroom-sized hourglass. He couldn't tell if he was remembering or forgetting to breathe. He felt confused, frightened: frozen. *How the hell does she do that — remind me of my dead wife?*

The gentle pad of the second tear resounded in his left ear. He was out of time.

Dad," she asserted despondently, "It's time for our morning walk."

Walter secretly loved their morning walks. It was October in Northeast Indiana, and the cool morning breeze would be sifting through the leafy color spectra of maple, elm, and oak. He envisioned himself wearing a faded gray windbreaker jacket and oversized jeans, his unwashed gray hair sticking out of his worn-out patriotic mesh hat, walking alongside her in the pale morning sunlight. She really was beautiful.

"Dad," she began. They both knew what she would say next. It was always two soft thuds and then the invitation for the morning walk. But if he remained silent for too long...

"We're all we've got," Walter finished her sentence hopelessly, echoing the credo slightly out of synch. He rolled over and pushed himself off the floor, rising from his bent knees before carefully straightening his stooped back. "I know pumkin," he said. "Let's go on our morning walk."

....

Walter still made her wait. She stood patiently in the silence outside his door. She used to protest such cold responses, but eventually conceded that they were necessary for him to process. It didn't really matter anyway; the silences were customary and she was content with the small level of engagement Walter might allow her throughout a given day. She was getting good at reading his silences, too. After two minutes and forty seconds, the lifeless, brown-green brass of the door handle slowly rotated, and the light of the hallway rushed forth to meet the darkness of Walter's room. He pulled the creaking door open, standing halfway-dazed, revealing his disheveled appearance tucked under his old mesh hat with the American flag embroidered in the middle. His eyes fixed upon the floor. He couldn't take her in all at once; it was too intense. She looked too much like his wife.

Sniffing and wiping her tears away she croaked, "Are you ready Dad?" failing to mask the pain in her voice.

She bends her right arm and sticks it out so I'll take it in my own. I act like I don't see her. "Let me get my jacket first," I say as I push past her and into the living room.

The living room was dim and smelled of dust. There was a weathered green couch on the side wall. On the back wall adjacent to the couch was a tattered leather love seat, holes showing its insides. It faced a heavy, old television set pushed back into a wooden entertainment center across the room. In the corner next to the love seat rested a ratty recliner made from worn green cloth over thirty years old, angled to either watch TV or grab a nearby book from the aging, wood chipped shelf. The coat rack leaned against the bookshelf, a dark wooden piece of collapsible who-knows-what, broken limbs serving as hooks bowing further under the light weight of autumn jackets. Walter headed straight for the coat rack and grabbed his wrinkly gray jacket, putting first his right arm in the sleeve then his left. He slipped his feet into his plain gray Velcro shoes, strapped them up tight, and straightened his back slowly to recover from his stoop. He zipped up his jacket and tracked her with his eyes as she entered the room. She wore a white undershirt underneath a tight pink blouse to cinch her small belly and accentuate her early forties' curves. A pair of navy blue jeans clung with little slack to her healthy thighs, traveling down into a pair of women's running shoes. He looked at her and smirked. She smiled at him and waited for him to say something nice to her.

"See how I take my fucking shoes off?" Bemused, he turned away from her frown and reached his bony hand toward the cheap, gold-painted knob. He twisted it and pushed it from him, the dirt-faded door opening to welcome a cool autumn breeze at the threshold. He left the door wide open as he walked down the cracked stone steps of his porch and onto the grass of his small, un-raked yard, stopping under the golden elm tree next to the street. Sensing her anxiety, he turned, beaming.

"Well pumkin," he motioned, "are you coming or not?"

She smiled, laughingly shaking her head in disbelief as she made her way down the steps and out onto the street. The pale morning light bounced off of the golden leaves and onto her. She laughed and wiped her dripping nose. Walter extended his hand. She took his hand in hers, and they started walking.

It was a long time before either one of them spoke. Walter shuffled along, his feet kicking up leaves. He wrapped his old arm in her soft warm bicep; his free arm traveled a stiff, crooked line down into his jacket pocket. He stared straight ahead. She tried to.

Every 24 seconds, she throws a transient glance my way.

Walter pretended not to notice, fixing his eyes straight ahead. The small neighborhood road was lined with autumn colored trees. After one last transient glance in the silence, a gruff voice with something dead inside of it says:

"You know, you look a lot like her mother."

She tightened, but it was almost imperceptible. Forcing a smile, she turned toward Walter and said, "I think you meant to say *'yer'* mother."

12

"Oh right, sorry," grumbled Walter. He looked to his right: he thought he saw something. He shook his head then gazed upward into the underside of an auburn maple canopy.

"Say," he offered, "it's getting close to the day she died." He took his hand out of his flimsy jacket and removed his patriotic cap, scratching his head with the bill. "Today's the tenth, so that means...well, what day was it again?"

"Mom died two weeks from today," she sighed. Walter knew that. He was just making sure.

"Do you remember her at all?" He stopped and turned his desperate gray eyes towards her. "Do you remember how your mother died?"

"I have vague impressions, really."

She stopped and gazed at the auburn maple tree. "I remember her comfort, her warmth. I remember that she had blue-gray eyes, just like me, and that everything she did was beautiful. I was really young, though, Dad, when she died." Walter's quiet, expectant gaze obliged her to continue.

"I remember Mom pulling me in the wagon to the park, the Red Ryder wagon, and playing on that playground," she added quickly, "and I can see her standing there over me, the sun to her back casting a shadow over me, making her glow and look big and important and pretty." She stopped, looking bashfully at the ground. "And I remember the last time I played in the leaves with you and her, right in our yard over there." She turned and pointed back in the direction of

Walter's house. Walter frowned, remembering the neighborhood maple as the site of their last autumn, not the yardside elm. He decided not to push.

"That must've been the September before Mom got sick," he mused.

"Yeah, it was," she sighed. "I remember being in the hospital, seeing Mom lay there and crying because she couldn't play with me. And then, I remember her funeral and seeing everybody crying and being really sad for a while." She turned her eyes to Walter. He looked to the ground.

"But Dad," she went on, "we've always had each other, and you're all I can remember. So everything we did without Mom...well, you made seem fun, and *normal*. You raised me, and I was happy, and I *am* happy." She turned toward the fall trees colored in pale fire lining the neighborhood street. "God", she laughed, "I wouldn't know what to do without you, Dad. What would my life be like? What would my *day* be like?" she added with a chuckle. She paused, her eyes set forward.

"I remember how lonely I was staying with Grandma when you went away to the war,"

What the fuck is she doing?

"....and when you came back,"

Why the fuck would she talk about that?

"....not the same,"

Why goddamnit, why?

14

"....wanted to help,"

STOP

"....forgiveness,"

JESUS CHRIST

"....I know you love me."

"....and I love you, and I am here to take care of you. I am always here to take care of you, and I will never leave you Dad." She turned to look at him, waiting in the silence.

"That's nice," Walter said to the leaves.

III

Used to be some nights I'd wake up covered in sweat, my tendons clenched, heart sore from pounding, fear in my blood and a black cloud over my bed until I count to three and come to. Now, every other night I wake up from this goddamn nightmare. I wake up and my mind is screaming but my mouth is mute and I freeze and I can't shake those awful fucking images out of my head. It feels so real every goddamn time — I can see my tendons bulging out of my young thick forearms as I extend my elbow forward, gripping a gun, and I can see every detail of how it's made: the grain of the handle and the smoothness of the barrel and how it all fits together, and it's so black it gleams in the sunlight as I plant it right on the forehead of a child, and the pores on her forehead give a little as I impress the gun barrel into her skull. I feel a heaviness surround me, I think it's fear, and I can feel it enclose me, pouring in slowly like soft whimpers in my periphery, the distinct smell of fire and flesh in the morning air, all under the pale yellow morning sun I love so much — and I think about how my wife is dead and how it's all my fault, and I think about my daughter with her blue-gray eyes. I press the gun barrel harder into the little girl's skull. I can see every last detail of the little girl's face — the contours, the lines and the structure, the color of her eyes and the way her hair looks, and I swear every time I'll remember, but I never do. Because it all turns to nothing, her face I mean. And then I blow her fucking brains out.

—and her nothing face turns to nothing cartoon noir black and white blood and splashes onto my army fatigues. And then the ground is moving, like I'm on a conveyor belt, and there's one of us every 24 feet or so, starin' up into the sky like fools until our eyes burn out, turning into white pools of liquid cornea dripping down my face, and I feel like someone is making us all look into the sun, someone wants me to forget—

"Hmm, interesting," remarked the doctor, his indifferent eyes peering over his glasses at his clipboard, "tell me more about that." Walter awoke to find himself sitting in his worn recliner, feeling nauseas and staring blankly at Dr. C, his lead psychiatrist.

You can do whatever the goddamnhell you want when you're on your own time, but when you're on someone else's, all ofa sudden its 9:00 and you're at your therapy session telling some goddamn finks your darkest nightmares—

18

"Nightmares? Plural?" Dr. C shifted in his seat, showing much more interest.

Goddamnitall to hell! They finally got inside my fucking mind!

"No, Walter," the great psychiatrist remarked with a doctoral sigh, "you're talking out loud."

"Oh." Walter remained slumped in his armchair, making his best attempt to not think. He envisioned the empty space in his head. The space was connected to an inter-cranial tunnel that had a small delta, pouring over his mind visions and memories from long ago, not all of them real. *Close the fucking floodgate*, he thought. *Jesus, I'm thinking again,* he added, before the words "Jesus, I'm thinking again" slowly dissolved into "Js I thnk" and finally a big mental "J" that got swallowed forever by the soft interlining of his skull.

Dr. C was quite successful. Regarding veteran mental care, he was the most renowned doctor in the Midwest. Much had to be done, many family sacrifices made, to procure his daily home visits for Walter. His program was legendary; it had been proven time and again to cure patients just like Walter. If he just regularly took his medication with breakfast at 8:00am — immediately preceding his morning walks — took a shower after breakfast, dressed himself in clean clothes and decided to open up during their 9:00am therapy sessions, interacted with his round the clock nursing staff — setting goals from 10:00-10:20am and doing activities from 10:20-11:50am — had lunch at 12:00pm, took an afternoon walk until 1:00pm, took a light afternoon nap before preparing for his in-home support group sessions on Mondays, Wednesdays, and Fridays starting at 3:00pm and ending at 4:30pm — volunteering at the animal shelter on Tuesdays and Thursdays during the same time frame — ate dinner at 5:00pm, watched television from 5:30-6:30pm, wrote in his journal from 6:30-7:59, drank a glass of water with his medication at 8:00pm, and did some light reading before his 8:30 bedtime, he'd be cured. If he followed a similar regimen on Saturdays and Sundays, allowing for supervised free time from 3:00-4:30 (because, of course, neither does group therapy meet nor is the animal shelter open on the weekend), he'd be cured.

Dr. C knew exactly how to treat Walter. Even the patient's family agreed with his methods.

The problem was, Walter didn't want to be treated.

"Walter, what do you think your nightmares are telling you?"

They're telling me I've been through hell, that my wife died cause I wasn't smart enough to know anything was wrong or rich enough to buy her a cure, that I've lived a goddamn war

and nothing will ever change that — not that I really want it
to; that when I came back from the war I felt like I was dead, I
was dead from what I had seen and done, and that somewhere
sometime on that line while I was away my daughter died too,
and it was all my fault. Sometimes I feel like I killed her, we
were so close cause we only had each other, and after my soul
died from what I had done, I brought her down with me, I
killed her — and now I have to live with the daily reminders of
this goddamn tragedy, with no peace, no freedom, no way to
pay what I owe and a bunch of fucking black suited wolves
outside my home and their goddamn white coated rats
crawling through my floorboards and into my life and through
my memories, gnawing away at my goddamn sensibilities and
leaving their traces all over my reality, their fucking bite
marks and scratch marks and fucking turds all over my home
without wiping their goddamn grimy little claws — tearing at
me because I'm a true American, not like these bastards, these
communist-capitalist-fascist-fags that want to take me down,
these government bureaucrats fucking their big business
buddies coming into my home to bring me down because I
know what I know, these scrub-wearing conspiratorial fucks
that spied on me every goddamn day till they found out every
inch of my home and life and used it to bring me down because
I'm a true American that served his country and came home
and didn't get shit like the resta the vets — relied on my

*goddamn self to start all over again, all alone and start it all
over again goddamnit!*

Walter's eyes focused upon Dr. C's face. He and his
psychiatrist were approximately the same age, but the
doctor's face was much sharper. He had a crooked nose
capped by a neat gray-red mustache that curved downward
and gave away to a trimmed goatee. He had been balding for
years but was still holding onto some gray-amber hair he
kept regularly cut. His eyes were black and often expectant,
contemplative, or indifferent. At times, Walter thought he
detected coyness from the doctor, which he hated.

Dr. C was staring at Walter, amused.

Oh shit, what did I say?

"I think we're done here," smiled Dr. C. Walter snapped
upright, his two arms sliding down his legs to clutch his
knees, his neck and shoulders tensing. His psychiatrist
pretended not to notice as he finished writing his final notes
on the session. Walter felt heavy perspiration on his forehead
and the soreness of his old, gaunt fingers from gripping his
bony knees. His body grew feverish at the thought of
divulging the only secret he had left.

Did I tell them about...?

Tell us about what, Walter?" inquired his physician harmlessly, staring at his clipboard. Walter froze.
Fuck.

 Shit

  shit

     ...

"...Did I tell them about how I want ham salad on wheat for lunch goddamnit!" Walter groused, recovering quickly. The psychiatrist looked up from his clipboard with a quizzical brow.

"Here's what you can fucking do, you fucking goddamn eggheaded private eye motherfucker, you wanna help me all the goddamn time. Go in there and tell my *daughter* that I'm hungry as hell and that at 11:00 I better get a fuckingdamn ham salad sandwich on wheat with chips. And not those faggot pita chips neither, I want real goddamn American potato chips!"

The doctor stood up from his seat, tucking his clipboard under his left arm. He smiled warmly. "Ok Walter, I'll tell her."

....

Except you won't tell her what I fucking said, doc, because at 11:00 I don't find myself sinking my old yellow teeth into a lightly toasted wheat bread, down through the grains and into the wet crispness of sandwich lettuce shielding delicious ham salad spread, my lower jaw tingling from how savory the ham salad and the bottom toast are when its fresh and they're just melding together, real American potato chip crumbs all over my war veteran sweater — FUCK NO, I find myself with a belly gurgling hungry and unhappy painting a picture from the goddamn television set on a fucking how-to-paint show with a team of smiling idiot nurses fawning over the tiniest amount of effort I put into it.

This is the seventh layer of hell.

Daytime television and a bunch of grinning dumbasses. This is my 11:00. Every other goddamn day. A basic cable station, "Painting with Assholes", broadcasting from Fuck-Off, me holding my brush and playing the tortured artist like I'm fine but I just go crazy if anyone wants to see my work — in reality, I just don't give a damn about painting and I'm something awful at it so I just block their eyes from my canvas and they can't see that I haven't done a goddamn thing. I just go through the motions, but they can bet their candy asses I'm free somewhere deep in my mind, thinking how to make all of this go away. Sure, I squiggle a line here and there, one day might make a tree and even add a little bristly detail to its piney branches, maybe tomorrow paint an easy fall sunset, put my glasses on so I can look serious as I study the TV for technique — but I'm throwing them for a loop. Or at least, I'm trying to. It's kinda hard to be in control when you're running on a daytime television schedule broadcasting your personal hell at 11am.

I look up from the canvas, meeting the gazes of three young nurses surrounding me, their faces eager. "Give me some space, will ya?" I grumble. "You're crowding my genius." More like, you're crowding me from staring into this blank page to paint a mental picture of how to kill all of you. They all take two small steps back at the same time in a line, but keep watching me with those unctuous smiling faces. All I gotta do is last until 11:50, till they give me ten minutes to get ready for my lunch — and that ham salad sandwich will be a long time coming goddamnit — and judging by the particular song playing at this point in the episode, that'll be about 24 more minutes. That ain't bad.

...23 minutes and 58 seconds. Jesus Christ, Superstar.

I try not to think about the Suits outside. I look hard into the canvas and get lost in the subtle contour differences of where the paper may fold in some or be slacked a little more, made visible only by the dim light radiating dully from the dusty lampshade behind me. I tie up a few loose ends in my mind and lift up my paintbrush. I can see the giddy little fuckers holding their breath.

Walter touched the soft bristles to the white canvas, focused and pensive. The nurses let out imperceptible squeals of delight through their closed throats. He began painting what he thought was going to be another half-assed landscape.

Blue for the skies, a little gray too maybe...get some earth tones in there, some brown, yeah...

Brush bright with creativity and nostalgia, Walter worked.

Throw some, what is it? Auburn! Yeah, that's it, some auburn and burgundy — yep!

The nurses shot nervous smiles to each other as he painted, feeling a wary sense of accomplishment.

And a'course! A nice deep red for the uh, the uh...

Walter frowned.

...blood?

The nurses took a simultaneous line-step forward, concern

touching their faces along the shadows cast by the weak lamplight.

"BACK AWAY!" yelled Walter, hostile as he sprang toward the canvas and kicked it over, immediately falling down on top of it, clawing like a madman, tearing frantically at the image to prevent the nurses from seeing a single brushstroke. The nurses rushed forward, putting reassuring hands on his shoulders. "DON'T FUCKING TOUCH ME!" he threatened. They let go of him as he tore the remaining panel of canvas into incomprehensible shreds. He couldn't decide what made him angrier: actually engaging in his therapy as he was told or letting his guard down long enough to risk sharing secrets with his nurses.

The antique clock struck noon in twelve thin, tinny-brass chimes. Walter put his toes under his knees and placed his hands on the floor in front of him, attempting to push himself up. The nurses leaned in to help him onto his feet. Walter cursed, in part fighting the nurses while straightening his stiff legs to do the job alone, in part using their weight for assistance. When he was finally able to stand straight, he slapped away the supportive hands of the nurses like he had done everything by himself and brushed his dirty veteran sweater, smearing it with paint.

"Good people," he declared, "I've enjoyed today's session, but you've made me late for my lunch." He slapped his pants with limp wrists as if he was dusting himself off.

"And seeing as the highlight of my day is a ham salad sandwich and the low probability of eating real potato chips, *you better not fuck with me.*"

Walter sauntered into the kitchen covered in paint and hair a knotty gray mess, pants button popped off and left shoe untied. Sitting down across from an anxious daughter, he smirked and reached for his sandwich with fingerfulls of small cuts. He sank his old yellow teeth through the delicate balance of a well-layered lunch sandwich, thinking: *this tastes just like it should.*

Hell is over and I'm so goddamn hungry I'll even eat these pussy little pita chips.

....

It must be a Tuesday or a Thursday because my nostrils are full of stale pee and I'm finding myself standing over a scruffy pug, staring at his puffy asshole and wondering if those bastards put a probe up there to spy on me.

Guess I'm not much of a dog person.

Walter preferred cats. They were nonchalant loners. He admired their instinctual nature and their cool indifference. *I guess I could be a dog person, I mean, if I knew which ones were probed and which ones weren't. With cats, it's easy to tell. Hell, cats are so goddamn graceful — you can see it in the way*

they move their shoulder blades in smooth panther circles —
so it's easy to see if one has a probe up its ass, because it walks
like a goddamn four-legged robot and looks like an alien. But
dogs, that's a different story. They're all so fucking crazy and
lumbering and drooling, I can never tell. But I think this fella's
clean. Hell, maybe I could even like this old pug, bent over and
frowning, in need of a trim, quiet and alone in his thoughts.

Walter was at the local humane society, doing what Dr. C called "the community engagement" component of his therapy. He stood on the grounds, leash in hand, a lazy pug at his feet and an overcast October wind in his messy hair. It was a cold, depressing Tuesday, or maybe it was Thursday. He couldn't remember. Shivering in the fall wind, anticipating a dismal rain and trying to decide whether or not he could trust a pug, Walter was lucky. He was lucky to not have a weird indictment, and he was lucky to be allowed back in the humane society.

Walter was convinced that the only reason he was able to get out of the house for the community engagement component was so that the "agents" could give him relative freedom in exchange for lowered self-awareness and heavy regulation from complicit agents working undercover as humane society employees and volunteers. Or, in Walter's words, "*these 501c(3) motherfuckers are in on it.*" So, naturally, he surmised that some — "*but not all, because they gotta use some cute ones to fool me"* — of the animals were recto-fitted with surveillance devices. One day, his paranoia got the better of him, and he showed up donned in shop-class goggles and a pair of heavy latex gloves.

He could have been charged for animal cruelty with intent of bestiality. He could have been forbidden to enter the humane society ever again.

The workers wrote it off as a psychotic breakdown and welcomed him back the very next Tuesday or Thursday.

He was lucky.

Staring down at the fat wheezing pug — wondering if the dog knew that it and everything around it would one day die or even if it knew its rectum had just been inspected by a crazyperson — Walter didn't feel very lucky.

IV

She sat cross-legged outside Walter's door, a pair of
sleek glasses on her face, her hair tied back, studying. It
seemed like she always had to take her work home with her.
Walter made this process all the more challenging, to say the
least, but she managed to complete her professional reports
and plans in the small windows of time in which Dr. C felt it
safe to let Walter go unsupervised: at the beginning of the
day, in transitions between meals, and when going to bed.
The rest she did on the weekend. On Saturdays and Sundays,
Walter had "supervised free time" in lieu of
Monday/Wednesday/Friday in-home group therapy and
Tuesday/Thursday community engagement. Ideally, this
meant he was free to pursue any activity, as long as he was
monitored. Realistically, a typical Saturday or Sunday from
3:00-4:30pm would unfold to show her sitting in the hallway,
just outside of Walter's door, studying intently and not
thinking about how he was technically using "avoidance
tactics" by sequestering himself in his room.

Before she got worked up, she remembered to shrug.
She used to fight with him, demanding that he spend his free

31

time outside of his room and under her watch as advised by the doctor. In time, she grew tired of the altercations and compromised. If the doctor asked, she was "supervising auditorially."

At first, she dreaded leaving Walter alone. Now, she cherished the time. For one and a half hours on two days of the week, she could forget about him — absolve herself from this crazy old man who was supposed to act like a father. And, in the end, the free time was probably beneficial for Walter, too. She thought he deserved better than to be constantly "counseled" and "coached" through every choice. She knew the only way to be free was to stand alone, and she hated to see the proud old man stripped of his freedom.

Goddamnit, whadda luxury to just do my thing for once!

Walter stood in the abyss-colored blackness of his closet with foamy lips and a mouthful of warm, crisp beer. His aged, bent back leaned up against the crumbling closet wall; above, a decaying shelf bowing from the weight of a hodge-podge of old belongings almost touched the crown of his head. Antique beer cans cobbled the floor below, most of them finished and lined with semi-dried drops of golden rot, a few others remaining unopened. Above the beer cans were layers of trinkets, mementos, clothes, scissors, a Singing Billy Bass, a couple random coffee grinders, and God knows what else up to the ankles. Paint chips and cracked splinters, once yellowed time-tested stalactites, had fallen years ago and now were among the packratted keepsakes. The whole place smelled of mildew and dust. Walter shifted his feet, wading in the junk. His toe kicked one of the many old icepacks he had tucked into the somewhere of his closet, originally to ice the beer. He gave up on that idea over 20 years ago.

I don't care if it's warm, you can never go wrong with a classic American pilsner. Hell, I almost like it better warm. In the early days they woulda drank beer warm anyways, seeing as how refrigeration was a spotty thing. And when your only freedom's a dilapidated four by six closet, refrigeration is a spotty thing.

Walter lowered the can and tilted the body toward his strained squint. It was painted a fading aluminum gray. A smooth, fat red arrow draped down from the mouth, passing over the lipped indentation and running down thick and rectangular into a pointed head that stopped just above the navy blue block letters "ALL ALUMINUM CAN". A wide navy blue banner of the same hue wrapped around the body at the slightest angle, crossing over the fat red arrow halfway up the can. Just above the top edge of the banner ran the words "PREMIUM PILSNER" in thin white font. The center of the banner displayed the brewery's name in large, thick white letters, slightly narrowed for a touch of old world class.

"BEER" was printed neatly and much smaller underneath. Walter had already peeled the top off of the classic pull-tab can, revealing a large open mouth of white foam slowly dissolving into warm golden beer. After that, he separated the tab from the circular top of the can, putting each into their respective places in dusty piles on the opposite closet shelf.

Walter tilted his head back for another drink. He could feel the bubbles pop as the pilsner sloshed through the front of his mouth, into the front corners of his cheeks and lower lip, traveling over the tip of his tongue. He could feel the warm carbonation fizz and die as he pulled the draught over the back of his mouth and down his throat, leaving an aftertaste of golden hops, stale malt, and faint grain. Walter licked his lips. He lowered the can once more, closing his right eye in a cock-eyed attempt to enlarge his left, peering into the mouth of the can. In the darkness he could barely make out the bubbles rocketing upward to meet what was left of the foam, some popping and expanding into tiny ripples across the American-beer-gold surface, others sucking to the side of the can in a thin frothy line. *I'm gettin' pretty good at seeing in the dark,* thought Walter, raising the can to his lips, and *I always been good at drinkin' in the dark.* He smiled as he took another swig, welcoming the feeling of his throat choking down warm bubbles, gas leaving his eyes red. *Yep, there's nothing more American than a man like me drinkin' himself a premium beer from Kentucky. The way it's light but still full, bubbles with that soft biting corn, and you just go mow the lawn and drink a few and not feel a damn thing but good, standing there in the summer over your piece of freedom and your two sweet girls, July condensation coating a cold pull-tab aluminum can lightly crinkled in your calloused hand clutching it like the land of opportunity...*

She was still in the hallway, basking in her much-needed alone time. She smiled to herself, not thinking about what he was doing. She looked down at her reports; they were almost finished. She checked her watch. It was 4:06 — plenty of time before the next item on Walter's schedule.

Premium pilsners aren't for the Suits. The Suits are drinking wine and cocktails and coconut rums like a buncha terrorist queers. I'll stick to my warm American beer. Ain't like I got much choice nohow.

Walter slurped the last remnants of his favorite beer, crinkling the can some as he tucked it away. He wiped his wet lips on the forearm of his flannel sleeve, leaving the upper wrist of the shirt momentarily clean before using it to brush his beer stained whiskers. He paused, pondering to himself. Then, bending down backwards in the cramped closet and digging his right hand through the carpet of clothes and antique garbage:

It's probably about 4:06. I got time for one more.

V

Walter sat still in the dusty corner, shadows cast over his reclined body, green blanket across his legs, drooling slightly and presumably asleep. She looked up from her reading and cast her gaze towards him. He looked cute laying in his old-man recliner, worn black socks and stiff legs on the outstretched footrest, wiped out from a few hours of doing God-knows-what inside of his closet. Whatever he did in there, she didn't really care, because when she came running lightly across the hallway floor to catch the bedroom knob turn at 4:29 — Walter pulling the door slowly and stumbling out, wiping his slobbery lips and whiskers — he was in a good mood.

"What would you like for dinner, Evee?" he had asked her, planting a playful drooling kiss on her forehead, smiling as he tripped down the dim hallway and towards the kitchen. She followed him, an intrigued smirk on her lips.

From around the corner of the kitchen entryway came the sounds of rummaging and the opening and closing of pantry doors. She heard the suction cup of the refrigerator lining give way to a swinging door and the soft rattling of glass jars and condiments. She poked her head around the corner to satisfy her curious eyes, seeing Walter's baggy gray trousers hanging off the back of his bent rear, the rest of his body swallowed by the depths of the refrigerator. His mumbling was audible over the sound of moving and clanking and toppling: "Let's see here…"

She surveyed the kitchen: pantry doors wide open, pasta boxes and canned goods knocked over, a loaf of bread hanging over the precipice of the shelving like a sad, wheat-cracked accordion; countertops littered with produce, meat, sauces, spices, pots, plates, and pans; a small stream of running water pouring lazily onto a bowl of something in the sink. Feeling her soundless sigh, Walter jerked his body upward, banging his head on the underside of the refrigerator shelving, shaking its contents and knocking a pickle jar into an open parmesan cheese container. The parmesan fell over, landing flush on the end of the shelving and spilling sandy yellow-white cheese down Walter's wrinkled back. The cold grit of the cheese made him jump, and he bashed his head again on the shelving as the parmesan slid towards his butt crack. She ran over. Walter pushed himself out of the refrigerator and shut the door in a clumsy dash to keep anything else from falling out, straightening himself up quickly and throwing an armful of assorted food onto the nearest counter before nonchalantly reaching down his pants and brushing off his rear. He grinned, doffing his cap to her.

"Dinner tonight is my treat, pumkin."

She looked at Walter, unsure of whether she was amused or mortified. His half-deranged, cracked smile was contagious.

"Alright," she said, humoring him, "but please, Dad, wash your damn hands." She winked at him and left the room, hearing clanging and banging as she sat down on the couch to focus on her work report. Walter's cussing, tabletop pounding, and the sporadic sizzle of the frying pan or gurgling of boiling water made it hard. She kept reading, suppressing her urge to get up and hawk him in the kitchen. She was working on gaining more trust.

When Walter finally called her in, she was glad she had waited. Two plates of homemade beef and noodles with mashed potatoes sat on the table, steam rising slow and thin in the kitchen light, Walter beaming in a mangled apron.

"Mom's old recipe!"

She smiled and sat down. They ate together: talking, laughing, and truly enjoying one another's company. When they finished, he even sprang up to do the dishes. Had she not insisted he go watch the evening news to stay on his regimen, he would have cleaned the entire kitchen — or tried to, anyway. He settled into his familiar spot in his worn chair in the dusty corner of the living room, staring blankly at the television set and, the gentle sound of water running over ceramic floating to him from the kitchen, drifted off.

Now, all quiet and calm, she found relief in the fading day and its lack of apparent incident. She smiled at Walter as he slept in his recliner. *It's been a great Sunday*, she thought before returning to her reading. Everything was silent, still.

"SHIT!"

Walter rocketed upright in his chair, the raucous creak of the footrest locking into place underneath. He turned to face the window.

"Dad?" Startled, she threw her reading to the floor and gripped the couch, leaning forward in anticipation. Walter flicked a small opening in two creamy blinds with a boney finger and pressed his eyes to the window: "*A twig snapped in the rock garden! The Suits are doing a parameter check, the bastards!*"

The old man stared into nothingness. She watched him watch the darkness, her face stone-set, calculating. She was nervous, and she wasn't sure what she should do. She felt tiny beads of sweat form on her unflinching face as her mind raced with proper "strategies" and "treatments," her heart pounding through the silence. Walter sat still, his fingers in the same position between the yellowed blinds, a statue of a paranoid old vet.

And they were doing so well.

She stared through the dust suspended in the living room lamplight. Walter was motionless, but his scowling eyes were alive and vigilant. She was failing him. Her heart slowed from its manic beat to a sad march. She wanted to cry but knew it would make too much noise. Feeling a lump in her throat as she took in the old man's tragic image, she shook her mind in despair, her head remaining still. *What would the best daughter do in this situation?* she mused, frowning. The antique clock ticked, its usual gentle reminder of passing seconds seeming loud and obnoxious in the hushed living room. She thought about all of her training.

She was well aware that Dr. C would know precisely how to handle such a situation, but it was her duty to take care of it. She knew she had to comfort Walter in his duress, alone, to shoulder the burden and love him unconditionally, to control.

Is that really what would be best for my father? she thought. She searched hard, trying to separate obligation from emotion from insecurity. Her most important task was to be a good daughter, to make the best choice for Walter at any given moment. Sometimes that involved a relentless drive for control, a prerogative she had as the omnipresent family member. Tonight, however, the best choice was to let go, to trust in the therapy — to give Dr. C a call. He would know what to do.

She rose from the couch, hoping her knee wouldn't crack and snap the void. She positioned her back toward the door carefully, eyes remaining fixed on Walter, soundlessly edging out of the room. She reached the threshold to the kitchen and quietly turned to enter, sliding her hand into her pocket for her cell phone without making any noise and

"DON'T YOU FUCKING DARE."

She froze.

"DON'T YOU FUCKING DARE CALL THAT QUACK BASTARD," warned Walter, shadowed and motionless, still glaring through the tiny slit in the blinds.

"I KNOW WHAT YOU'RE UP TO."

She took her fingers out of her tight pocket, turning around slowly. "Dad—"

"YOU THINK I DON'T KNOW? YOU THINK I CAN'T TELL? YOU THINK I CAN'T SEE YOU USIN' THAT GODDAMN GOVERNMENT SATELLITE CELL PHONE TO WARN 'EM AS SOON AS I SPOT 'EM?"

She sighed. It was worse than she thought.

VI

"I don't fucking know why, I just do it!"

I'm so fucking angry, staring into the eyes of this phony old piece of shit playing the part of a self-aware dingbat — able to analyze his day and his fears and make an action plan, reaching over to pat you on the back during the hard parts when it's your turn to share, the pompous prick with his wrinkly face and wise eyes and wizard smile.

"That's why it's a fucking nightmare, because it's scary and unknown and your brain wants it to be that way. So I ain't supposed to know. I ain't supposed to know shit. And I tell you what else: you ain't supposed to be here, none of you. None of you assholes, but you know what? You're still here. You're still here, asking me about dreams and holding me accountable for goals I don't give a shit about, clapping your hands together in sad nursing home death applause for each other when you don't shit your pants for a day, reminding me to take my pills like a game of geriatric peer pressure mindfuck teacher's pet medicine man BULLSHIT—"

"Walter," warned Dr. C.

The patient was leaning forward in his green recliner, his left arm clutching the belly of his t-shirt, his right arm waving in the air with limp wrist and stiff fingers, bits of spit collecting at the sides of his madman mouth.

I'm so fucking angry. I must be at one of my tri-weekly therapy sessions.

"Walter, these people have come a long way to visit you in your home, to celebrate your successes and build you up through your struggles," Dr. C pointed out with a gentle frankness, "they deserve your respect." Walter's psychiatrist tilted his head in anticipation, raising an expectant brow. Walter surveyed the room.

Jesus Christ, who are these people?

—Like this old maid in the corner, how's she gonna tell me how to live when her hair's all over the place, wearing an unwashed blue sweatsuit with the top too small and her flabby 70s belly hanging out and the red embroidery saying "Grandma" when I'm pretty sure she doesn't have any grandkids.
—Or take this old bald bastard, blowing his own breath on his barren face, twitching his skin around his eye and winking like a fly keeps landing on his cheekbone, never looking you in the eye when he's talking to you, dilated pupils always chasing the

invisible bug.

—Or this old coot, wearing red and black flannel pajamas partway unbuttoned with his fuzzy lichen gray chest hair hanging out, bent over his chicken-bone knees to show the crown of his bald head with gray hair on the sides sticking out every which way like the picture of pure lunacy, babbling barely audible and counting on his fingers, counting, counting, always counting.

And then there's this motherfucker, the self-righteous psycho with his benevolent wizard smile, like he knows something I don't, like he wants to help me if I would only try but I won't give him the satisfaction of letting him teach me something because I know he doesn't know shit. Look at him — smiling over there like this all means something, his square jaw and chiseled face with just a little age-fat-and-wrinkle looking good after all these years because his eyes ain't got as much pain as mine, well dressed in a gentleman's polo sweater and nice khakis, psychotherapy success story, congratulatory and happy and believing —

Where do they find you crazy bastards?

"Walter," began Robert, the patient with the comforting smile, "if I may, doc," he finished, throwing a respectful glance towards Dr. C. The psychiatrist responded with furrowed brow, pursed lips, and a wave of the hand as if to say "of course!" Robert shifted giddily with Dr. C's approval before refocusing on Walter.

"Walter...."

Robert's smiling and waving his hands excitedly, explaining to me how I'm soo close to a breakthrough, but it's all muffled because I can't hear the asshole over the sound of my own thoughts screaming at him for being an opportunistic, moment-taking sonofabitch. And then he's plain mute to my ears because I'm yelling, "STOP PATRONIZING ME WITH YOUR SMILES AND YOUR NODS AND YOUR GODDAMN BELIEF SYSTEM!" but he keeps talking. Even after I've sprung out of my chair, jumped on his happy ass and put my fingers around his throat, he's still saying something about "trust in the therapy" and "love yourself" — even while I'm choking him to death.

Walter sat still in his recliner, his eyes fixed on Robert, visualizing a few poorly conceived plans and their undesirable outcomes. He shook his head, opting for silent indignation instead.

I turn and watch Dr. C watch Robert, the drone of Robert's voice fuzzy and distant. The doctor's looking at him, all

*interested and what not as Robert looks right at me and talks
about "fear" and "happiness" and "choices." Dr. C: give me a
fucking break. With your goddamn Freudian face and your
fake interest and your know-it-all academia blow it out your
ass advice, hanging your experience over my head to make me
feel small, raising your eyebrow and asking questions and
playing the game and using your expertise to make me feel
unfamiliar until you control the conversation and the moments
and then I'm on the other side of them, walking too far out on
the plank. I'm on the other side of everything, and you and the
fucking lunatics you surround yourself with are all watching
me inside my head watching you hold facial expressions and
I'm screaming a million things in my head but thinking nothing
at the same time, on the other side of everything and
wondering how they can buy all of this bullshit just like you
want them to, exactly what you say with blind faith, and then
suddenly I'm the crazy one, and Robert touches my knee
knowingly and says "I was there once," and no matter what I
do from then on I'm fucking wrong, but I sorta don't feel like
being right neither.*

Walter turned to fasten his eyes on Robert's cracked lips as
they took the form of his last words, his tongue articulating
them against his teeth. Walter saw them more than he heard
them, half-visualizing the letters seep out of Robert's mouth:

"....we support each other."

Robert, the smiling good guy who says he understands but probably doesn't.

"....we take care of each other."

Robert, the guy who believes and follows the plan, the successful one who buys in.

Walter looked around, soaking it all in.

—Who is this guy in the black and red flannel, senile, finger-counting, mangled hair?
—Who is this lady and who the fuck licensed her to wear that sweater?
—Wouldn't you have thought this old bastard would've gotten that fly by now?

I'm screaming a million things in my head but thinking nothing at the same time, on the other side of everything.

"None of you were in a goddamn war," I finally say, soft and broken.

Dr. C tilted his head, intrigued. Tears welled in Robert's eyes. The old man in the flannel stopped counting. "Grandma" leaned forward, respectful and engaged. Even the old bald fly-catcher quit blowing on his face and gave Walter his best attempt at eye contact. Taken aback, Walter looked down at the floor, genuinely apologetic.

"I'm sorry," he mumbled.

"No!" yelled Dr. C in delight. Walter raised his head.

"This is great! Keep sharing, keep sharing: it's all part of the therapy!" Dr. C nodded, eyes wide with approval.

I look at all the grinning fools surrounding me and know I'm too far on the plank.

....From somewhere far away, Walter could hear his voice playing into Robert's comforting smile.

VII

The pale morning sun spilled onto their shoulders as they held hands through the October dew, casting a soft glare on the memory. Walter's daughter walked thoughtfully alongside her father, her four-year old frame with light pink jacket and ponytail surrounded by an angelic sunlit glow. Her beautiful blue-gray eyes looked up at him in that mix of glassy wide-eyed adulation and wonder that children have for their parents, adorably magnified by a pair of oversized glasses. She kicked through the colorful dead leaves in a tiny pair of light up shoes, trying to keep up with her father's lazy blue-jeaned strides. He had a gray jacket — somewhat worn but still showing its nylon sheen — draping from his strong square shoulders. His scrawny neck and well-defined jaw were dotted with brown stubble. A mesh hat with an embroidered American flag in the middle sat atop a head of fading brown hair. His eyes were deep gray-blue; pain was in them, but not as much.

Walter stared straight ahead along the row of beautiful autumn-painted maple, oak, and elm lining his street, the rich sounds of rustling leaves and little feet in his ears. Every two-dozen seconds or so, he shifted his glance down to his daughter and her soft glowing eyes. They were unfathomably deep, blue-gray with a surreal gleam. People told Walter that she had her father's eyes, but only after her mother died. He looked away.

He fixed his eyes on an auburn maple. It was somewhat young but still a good height, beginning to fill out with rough, deep brown bark. Walter traced its trunk about twenty feet up to its thinning auburn canopy. The green-brown grass around the tree was carpeted with dead leaves. Walter watched as the October breeze plucked a maple leaf off one of the thickening limbs, leaf holding on at first but finally falling zen, swirling to its death like a pretty burgundy fire.

"Dad," said his daughter. Walter turned to see her big round eyes staring up at him. They were sparkling with pensive worry, as if she struggled with the gravity of her coming words.

"Yes, Evee?" he croaked, fearing her question.

"Where did Mom go?"

The moment unfolded around him on an indefatigable timeline that connected his anxious, burning gut to his cracked voice to his daughter's expectant eyes to the small, beautiful tragedy of an insightful child's answerless question. He could feel the edges of his sight blur, the trees fading into darkness. Heaviness slowly poured around from all sides, compressing his reality into an inward retreat with a tiny window to his daughter's worried eyes.

"She..." he could hear the distant shake of his own voice, far removed from the heavy darkness. He struggled to find the right words.

It had been one year since her mother died. She suffered through rounds of cancer treatments before deciding they were hurting her family too much. She didn't want to leave Walter raising Evee in a debt-ridden life of limited options. More importantly, she wanted the ability to spend her remaining time the right way — not weak and nauseated in a hospital gown for her loved ones to see. She wanted to be the warm and affectionate mother, not the dying burden. She wanted to play with Walter and Evee in the leaves, and maybe last long enough to carve pumpkins one more time.

When she passed, Walter felt guilty.

If only I coulda done better, had a better job or even tried to borrow the money, my little girl would have a mother.

She tried to explain it to him. It was for his sake. It was for their daughter's sake. For the last bit of her life, she said, she wanted to be *present.*

Goddamnit, I didn't fight hard enough.

Walter gazed into his daughter's eyes, thinking about time and how it dropped him off answerless to a sweet sad daughter.

There was something I coulda done.

Truthfully, Walter didn't know where his wife went. He didn't know about life and God and death and what it was all for. After she died, he tried not to think about it anymore.

"To be honest with you Evee," Walter said, the October trees becoming sharper, the darkness fading but leaving the imprint of heaviness on his chest, "I'm not sure where Mom went. But I do know that she's safe now." Walter exhaled and looked at Evee, wondering if he had said too much.

She smiled. So did Walter.

"Well, as long as Mom is safe." She grinned with childlike wisdom. Her joyful cheeks pushed her glasses up higher into her eyes as she showed her tiny teeth with their tiny gaps. Walter felt the heaviness in his heart turn to warmth. He was happy. He loved his little girl.

"But don't you go anywhere Dad," she added, turning to face the October morning road. "We're all we've got."

VIII

Walter's eyes grew weary as he looked up at the crumbly ceiling from under his old quilt. The window to his bedroom was open, autumn wind flowing through the mesh window screen, twisting past the metal bars that kept him from escaping. Walter and his warm blanket welcomed the soft chill of a perfect fall night, his head gently impressed on the pillow, his arms peacefully folded on his chest, his legs heavy and body sleepy.

His eyes started burning from the staring, but he couldn't close them. He rolled to his left side and gazed out the window. The sound of scattering dead leaves called to him, followed by an orchestra of rustling, wind-blown trees. By moonlight he could see the multicolored ocean of rippling leaves clinging to their shadowed limbs. Walter loved the moon. The quilt was getting hot.

Walter shifted again, returning to his back, his eyes calibrating until they focused onto the same patch of ceiling. He inhaled deeply, then sighed. His folded hands returned to his beating heart, and he tried to think about nothing. All he thought about was the comforting chill of a moonlit Indiana night. He had to get outside.

It was late. His bedtime had passed hours ago.

And a'course, she's here to check up on me.

He didn't have sure feet in his old age, and sometimes he talked to himself. His bedroom window was clad with metal, and all of the household doors were heavy, old, and noisy. The prospect of sneaking out and back in undetected was next to impossible.

The wind howled, quiet and short, but with longing. He sighed at the thought of being a grown man and having a bedtime, becoming indignant as he mused. He snatched the underside of the covers with his right hand, yanking them off and to the floor in one motion. He lay still, brooding for a second in the shallow darkness of his room. Then, he sat up slowly, carefully swinging his legs off the side of the bed. His bony legs dangled over the floor momentarily before he eased toes, balls of his feet, and heels onto the carpet. He shifted his weight forward until he was standing up as straight as his crooked body would allow, remaining still in the soundless dark of his bedroom. He listened for any extra noise — muffled voices, a television, footsteps — that might be of use to him and his mission. The house was unusually silent.

Well old man, that means two things. The good news is,

she's most likely asleep. The bad news is, your old ass shuffling across the floorboards'll be fucking loud as hell.

Walter stood, weighing out his choices. He cocked his head up and to the left, paused in thought, then cocked his head down and to the right.

I'm gonna have to just walk right out, but I'm gonna need some sounds to cover me.

He wrinkled his brow, concentrating deeply on a spot on the lower wall.

Think old man, think...
   ...

     ...

       ...

        Yergoddamn right!

Walter noticed the furnace vent for the first time.

This old house and its rickety heater, God bless it. All I gotta do is wait for it to come on...

Walter remained motionless on the old carpet of his room. He waited for the furnace to kick its jumbled parts into place then trumpet its loud background rush of hot air throughout the house. If he walked quietly enough, the furnace and its noisy bedroom vent next to her pillow might swallow the sounds of his escape. Walter estimated that the furnace would be on for the duration of about eleven minutes before shutting off, and it would cycle back on after about thirteen. He figured that it had turned off around the time he noticed the bare silence of the house, which was about six minutes ago. He resolved to keep standing still for the remaining seven minutes.

The wind let out its baritone howl. Walter felt it sweep across his feet and dance up his body, tickling his unshaven whiskers. The caress of the breeze forced him to notice that his stiff joints had been aching. He bent his knees slightly then straightened them again. He did this a few more times before he realized that the vibrations of his almost imperceptible calisthenics may become a whiney floorboard creak somewhere else in the house. He froze. He felt like he could hear his bones crack into place.

The hoot of an owl — he darted his eyes to the window.

He could see the breeze pour through like soft river waves. His eyes flitted to the shadowed door. *Can I hear her breathing?* He listened as his eyes bore into the dark oak, half-dazed but focused intently, the moment heavy and ringing in his ears. He couldn't hear the owl's second call through his concentration. His legs were tightening again, and a dull ache in his lower back sharpened with the passing seconds. He squinted his eyes and shifted his head forward a half of an inch. He didn't hear anything. *Just my imagination I guess.* Regardless, he stayed statuesque, his eyes burning from their unblinking stare, the darkness gnawing at the edges piece by piece until all that was left was the shadowed oak. Alone in the dark, staring at the grisly bedroom door and wondering at the horrors it guarded, he couldn't remember if he had gotten out of bed.

This could be a dream. One horrible fucking dream where I open the door and see something terrible I don't wanna but I hafta...

Walter attempted to visualize beyond the door, but couldn't. The sound of nothingness droned in his ears; the darkness weighed upon him.

...Then, he heard it.

From far away came the sound of clicking metal followed by a low muffled rumble. The tinny kick-start of the furnace ticked and banged through the hollow duct until the loud ambience of rushing heat poured out from the vents. Walter smiled at the door. His cover had arrived.

He began sliding his right foot forward. Pain shot from his tendons into his lower back, and he remembered that his joints needed some limbering.

Careful. Another sloppy move like that and you'll be the sound of an old man falling on the floor.

He cautiously bent his knees then straightened them again. He twisted his trunk to either side but could barely turn his body. He did the same for his neck. He then bent his back forward slightly — which was more than he cared to — and straightened it again, feeling an uncomfortable pop.

Walter rubbed his aching back, bent low and shuffling forward, pain in his body. *The moon'll take care of that*, he thought, reaching for the door knob even though ten feet away, moving slow with yearning arm outstretched.

When he finally reached the door, he wrapped his hand around the worn brass knob, its coldness passing along his fingertips and sliding smoothly into his palm as he prepared to turn it. He moved his wrist to the right, slow and painstaking, the cold knob turning with his clutched hand. He could feel the small vibration of each splinter hitting the lock as it slid out of the wooden frame and into the door. If he pulled the door inward, even a hair, there would be no turning back. He stopped.

What if my cover's no good?

Knob tight in his hand with the door nearly open, he began to second-guess his plan.

You old fool. You need more than just a furnace to cover your pathetic arthritis shuffle.

He devised a new plan.

So I loosen my grip on the knob and let it slide back into place, about-face without lifting my heels, slide my socks across the floor and crawl my ass to bed. I fall asleep. I can't remember if I have a nightmare or not — I probably do but it's not important. The next day I wake up early, the sun shining, and get to work. I dirty up alla my weekday clothes. All of 'em. I wipe my ass with 'em, I blow my nose with 'em, I spill my breakfast on 'em, whatever. I save everything all up and it's right before bed and I gotta pile fulla dirty clothes that bitch has to wash and dry, so late she'll fall asleep with the washer and dryer on, and when she looks at me with those worried tears and asks me why I just make up some bullshit psychotic reason and then go to bed, and I wait for her tired eyes to leave

*the laundry room and fall asleep, and those raucous ass pieces
of shit will be enough background noise for me to sneak out...*

Get a grip old man.

Walter felt the cold knob growing warmer in his sweaty
palm. He didn't know what to do.

How about I...

He searched the door for answers. It was quiet and
indifferent.

No. But what about...?

The autumn breeze licked his pajama-bottomed legs. He had
to get outside.

At all costs.

Walter tugged softly at the handle, cringing as the door came
swinging open in time with a long, brittle creak. He pulled the
door the rest of the way open to kill the noise, revealing the
dark hallway. He poked his head out and surveyed the
corridor neurotically, his ears anticipating the sound of
footsteps and open bedroom doors. Everything was quiet.

Walter raised his right leg and extended it across the threshold of his room, pointing his stiff foot and inching it over the hallway carpet. He lowered his toe down toward the floor. He tightened his face and clenched his teeth as he watched his toe ease toward the carpet, waiting for the blast of a bomb or the wail of a high-powered security alarm as soon as he made contact.

He felt his toe connect with the carpet, give a little, then gradually flatten to allow his heel to plant underfoot. With one foot awkward and undecided in either room, he closed his eyes and swung his left around less cautiously to join his right.

He opened his eyes to find himself a few feet from his room, standing in the middle of the hallway. He scanned the corridor. It looked the same, only darker. He turned to his left and shuffled toward the living room. He could see the spots that would creak underfoot and was careful to avoid them. Considering his short, flat steps and his ebbing dexterity, it took a while.

Like a goddamn minefield out here!

The aging family pictures lining the wall had an eerie moonlit glow partly obscured by fallen midnight shadows. Everything felt long and heavy. He feared he may be going too slow, but reasoned that he could spend more time in the hallway if it meant not being heard.

Yep, sometimes you just gotta hide right out in the open...

Walter circumvented the deadspots inch by inch, slow and soundless. His eyes began to make out the outline of the living room. He could see the side of the couch where she sat with her reading in the evening. The couch became steadily larger in his view in time with his slow scoot, more and more of the space around the couch becoming visible, too.

His knee stubbed the armrest with a soft bang, telling him he had reached the entrance to the living room. He froze in horror, imagining a cavernous echo ricocheting around the living room walls and into his daughter's bedroom. The night lay still and quiet.

Walter turned his head toward the house door. He stared at the carpet in front of him. The space between him and the door grew in his eyes.

It's a long walk across the dusty carpet to freedom.

All else drowned in the sound of the furnace as he made his way to the door. He extended his hand, even though he was still fifteen feet away from the exit. The pace of his shuffle quickened as his heart raced. He was even more exposed than before. The weight of his angst grew with each step, amplified by a preemptive giddiness as he envisioned his calloused hands enclosing around the cold doorknob.

I grab the handle and turn it gently.

Walter paused.

Was it really that easy?

He closed the door silently behind him, standing alone on the porch steps in the October night. He took each step one at a time, quietly — not so much from fear anymore, but more out of respect for midnight and its solitude. He looked up at the yellow gibbous and could see the remainder of its ethereal outline. The chill of autumn washed over him, and he realized he was still in his pajamas. He didn't care. The cold breeze felt good. He followed the light of the moon down to his yard, looking out across it.

Shadows loomed in his periphery. He looked to his right, seeing two black Impalas parked under a distant streetlamp. He shook his head and they disappeared.

Oh, they're out there alright.

He shifted his gaze back over his yard, toward the small

gravel driveway near the corner of his home. There was an old tree glowing dark in the night. It leaned up against the side of the house — its roots were starting to crack the foundation some. He turned and faced the tree, squinting from the grass just off the stoop. His vision followed its trunk up to its split limbs, rustling fingers fading into blackness above the roofed corner of his house. Walter pondered in the whistling wind.

Yep, they're out there somewhere — but I don't give a damn.

Autumn frosted grass crunched softly under his socks as he started walking. His feet were damp by the time he reached the driveway. Dirt and small pebbles clung underfoot as he trudged across the gravel, indifferent to the jagged edges of the rocks. If anyone looked out the window on this October eve, they would see a crazy old man in his pajamas walking shoeless through the cold — hair unkempt, body stooped, plodding with deranged determination towards a twisted trunk of shadows.

Walter neared the corner of his house, passing a cobwebbed outdoor light near the garage. Its motion sensor light stopped working long ago. Walter chuckled.

To cover their tracks they gotta cover mine.

He imagined he heard the soft trigger of the floodlight, but the darkness prevailed.

Maybe they could catch this old coot, but they'd rather catch 22 instead.

Walter smiled in the darkness and continued to the corner of the house, his socks rustling through the leaves at the base of the old tree. He looked up the trunk, his eyes stopping at a branch hanging over his little one-story home. For the first time since closing the door and greeting the autumn night, fear tugged at his insides. He traced the limb back to the tree's knotted torso, down along its trunk to its roots, through the small patch of grass and to his wet socks.

Been at least thirty years since I climbed this here tree...

Walter doubted himself. He could hardly tie his shoes anymore, let alone scale a tree. Moreover, if he *really* wanted to see the moon, once up the base of the tree he would have to inch out along its limb and transfer onto the roof of the house without making any noise. It was next to impossible.

He turned to look at the yellow moon through the branches. The wind whispered to him through the leaves. *Sorry moon, but there just ain't no way.* He turned and looked back at the house. The door invited him to return to his bed.

He knew he'd be safe and warm in his home.

What am I doing out here?

His heart was tied to a string that ran back over the driveway, across the yard, through the door and into his bed. Walter knew he wasn't where he should be.

I don't belong here....

The wind pushed Walter into the tree with a sudden chilling gust. His head lolled backward but was caught by a few worn and overlapping edges of bark, putting his eyes in direct line with the moon as the twittering tree fingers parted in the wind to give him a better view. Staring at the moon, Walter didn't know if he was in fear or in awe, or even if there was much difference.

They come from the same place, fear and awe. The only difference is where they take you. One of 'em takes you back and the other draws you forward.

He turned to face the tree once more, studying the grooves in the bark. Even in the darkness, he knew every detail. He extended his right hand upward and grabbed a seemingly invisible knot with his bony, arthritic fingers, picking up his right foot and sticking his toes into a notch a few feet above the roots. He paused for a moment. He was horrified, but knew his fear would pass.

Yep, just as soon as I finally start climbing this goddamn tree...

He pulled himself up with his right hand, his left leg searching for a known foothold, his left arm partway around the tree, clinging for balance. His old bones ached as he pulled and hoisted himself up to a lower branch just under the limb that extended over the house. His knees cracked when he tried to stand up on the low branch; stumbling momentarily, he reached both arms up, grasping at nothing and losing balance, one second of fear consuming him until his waving hands closed around the upper branch. His knuckles looked ghastly in the moonlight as he clung with both hands, his aging shoulders burning, his knobby knees growing weak. He would have to rely on his dying upper body strength to pull himself up.

He looked down at his socks, his toes and heels hanging over the yard. He considered climbing down, but knew that it would actually be harder than progressing up the rest of the tree. He was past the point of no return.

It's just something you gotta do. It gets easier the further you go.

Walter pulled with all his strength, kicking his legs in the night, clamoring up the branch. After a cumbersome struggle, he hoisted his upper body up and over the branch with his legs still dangling in the air, the limb cutting into his gut. All of his weight was on his belly, flab hanging over both sides of the branch as it pushed into his diaphragm and stifled his breath. He hung there in comfortable pain, his stomach his new center of gravity, his stiff palms pressed into the bark for balance. Walter tried to catch his breath, but his position made it difficult. Even so, he was relieved to be where he was, waiting in the silence, suspended in the dark.

Pause...

Walter tried to pick up his right leg and raise it to the branch. It was loose in the wind, disconnected and far away. He concentrated on the neurons traveling from his brain and to his leg in order to complete such a task. They were slower than he remembered, having to take detours through his crooked and ailing body, but they eventually reached his foot. He twitched his toes some before rolling his right ankle in the air and gaining control of his lower right leg. He then bent his knee and flexed the right of his groin to raise his bony leg parallel to the branch. Taking great caution, he pivoted on his stomach and dropped his right leg onto the other side of the limb, straddling the branch facedown, clutching it like a delirious lemur. He shimmied forward carefully, his body pressing hard against the limb as it began to bow under his weight. He passed overhead of the yard, his moonlit shadow falling over the gutter. He inched forward, hovering over the edge of the slanted roof.

Almost there...

He was nearing the end of the branch, staring at the roofing and calculating his dismount, reaching tentative hands forward then snapping them back to clutch the limb, the skinny bone of the branch bending further and further under his weight in his quiet panic. Suddenly, the end of the branch snapped and the roofing became bigger and bigger in his eyes until he hit his face on the shingles with a sickening thud, his left arm pinned underneath him as he rolled onto his back, sliding in terror toward the edge of the roof, bracing himself for his death.

His left foot fell into the gutter with a raucous clang, the friction of the shingles catching the rest of his body and keeping him from falling. For a long time, Walter lie sprawled on the slanted roof, thinking he was dead.

....Then, his old fears returned, and he knew he had to be alive.

His sore back ached with the dull pain of embarrassment. He was certain he'd been heard. He waited for sounds of stirring in the house below — doors opening and closing, her footsteps and gentle clatter — anticipating the porch light in his periphery and the sinking feeling of his silence when she finally discovered him.

His eyes were at the stars. The darkness consumed him. He lay still, arms and legs stretched wide, one foot in the gutter, gravity softly tugging from the roof's edge. The wind passed over his arm hairs, making goosebumps and filling his ears with howls and swooshing leaves. He lay fretful and unmoving, like a child who feigns sleep in the early morning darkness minutes before mother sounds the alarm.

They're coming.

Walter waited. His mind raced, but the darkness swallowed his phantasmal thoughts. He listened to the wistful cry of the October wind for a while before realizing that nobody was coming.

And if they are, who gives a damn?

Walter smiled. An indescribable warmth crept inside his body, radiating from his core and into his veins, growing exponentially until his whole being was the soft glow of happiness. He wondered how many nights his fears had killed.

Is being free really this easy?

The moon was ablaze with celestial light. He didn't know how to get down, and he didn't really care.

IX

Walter tore his quilt away, gasping. He was saturated in sweat and it was beginning to stain his sheet and old feather mattress. He stared at the ceiling, feeling feverish. Terror gave way to excitement as he recalled more of his nightmare.

I'm looking at my defined tendons, clutching my pistol, the soft whimpering of death in my periphery, only now I can make out the faces of women and children, dirty and crying, a few men in the center, all watching me impress the barrel into the little girl's forehead. I look at her face and see every detail and contour and her little eyes, and I feel the skin of her soft forehead give a little bit when I push the barrel in harder and grit my teeth, powerful and fearful and its all the same, and right before I pull the trigger I hear a desperate voice cry out from the death, and then I blow her brains out and her little nothing face turns into black and white blood all over my clothes. But last night, it was different.

Walter lifted his calloused old hands, examining them from where he lay.

Last night, I dropped the gun in the dirt. Well, it's so bloody it slips out of my hands. I turn my palms and bend my fingers to look them over and my hands are soaked in red blood. RED BLOOD, like it's supposed to look. And then I'm looking at my hands in horror and the blood pools run over the cracks in my palms when I remember she had beautiful brown hair...

Walter could never remember this many details. He wanted to write them all down.

And I'm reaching for my pencil and pad but something stops me. The little faceless brunette has ahold of my arm, in my bed. Everything is real, the feeling of the mattress and my body sinking into it, my head down soft on the pillow with its worn folds around my skull, the outline of the bedroom as if my eyes were open — and then there's this little girl, sweet and beautiful and faceless, brown hair, holding onto my arm with a bullet hole in her head. I tell myself it's not real, and she fades away, and I lay there paralyzed, hearing someone's footsteps in the room and seeing shadows wander across my bed, and realize that if I did write something down they'dve seen it, the fuckers — and I lay there paralyzed before I realize I'm half-asleep and half-awake with haunting visions in my head and there's no girl and no pad and no nurses but just a heavy quilt and the 1..2..3 of my counting conscience as I clench my body and rock back and forth in my mind to wake up from my sleep paralysis and write all of my revelations down —

1...2...3!

1...2...3!

1...2...3!

Walter awoke in his bed, his eye's fixed on the same outline of bedroom, neck taught, heart pounding, tepid burn in his gut. Relieved, he strived hard to stay awake. He thought about the day ahead. He thought about breakfast, and how he could get out of taking his 8am pills. After lying still for six minutes, the slow drag of sleep pulled on his eyelids.

X

I don't have to read the paper to know what's going on.
I don't have to watch the TV to know this nation's at war.

We're a nation of war. We're a nation of war, all of us
screaming "Feed the Machine!" like a buncha pilled-up TV
burnouts needing someone else to look at instead of ourselves,
someone else to hate and blame and outcast for standing in the
way of progress so we can go about our daily lives with our
chocolates and our gasoline and our coffee, living a first world
life on last-world principles with third-world slaves only
knowing the words "Don't shoot" in English. Mothers and
daughters and wives, fathers and sons and husbands, brothers
and sisters and cousins who like to look up at a clear blue sky,
who have homey-kitschy knick-knacks and welcome mats, who
like to eat good meals in good company, and tell stories and
get wide-eyed, these people laugh too — and they might even
have a pet dog or cat or a worthless little goldfish the kids get
so excited over when he swims up to the glass — only knowing
the words "don't shoot", and maybe learning the words "Fuck
the Americans" as soon as you about-face with your high
powered automatic machine gun in your arms having just

destroyed their homes (tracking deathcaked mud all over their living room like a goddamn barbarian) and recede out the door, their eyes blurry with the color of government-issued camouflage and tears.

We do this every day in every corner of the world.

We have wars for land, wars for influence, wars for democracy, wars for oil, wars for peace for Christ sake, and the fat cats wave the back of their hand with a mouthful of fine food oozing out of their Jabba mouths down their double chins and onto their suits that their maids work to clean, saying "what's a few more pawns in the King's power play?" — when a pawn's not a pawn, it's a real life with a mortgage and a beautiful daughter back stateside living with unprepared grandparents clipping coupons and going without until Dad can come back home and work again, riding the school bus to a cold dark home with dusk shadows and unpaid bills and short social security checks, growing up fatherless, motherless, dreading every phone call and unannounced visitor, awaiting the return of the battleworn hero made crazy by a dead wife and a money hungry massacre. And this godforsaken shit kills another godforsaken brown man with the same daughter, the same poverty, the same whole life ahead of 'em with a puppet master behind for the same land, same influence and democracy and oil and sure as hell for the same peace, and for the same brokenness.

We're a nation of war.

*The machine doesn't stop: it can't stop. We've always had an
enemy and we always will. But America ain't just at constant
war with the nazis and the commies and the jihadis and
whoever we want to kill in between —*

> *the homeless man on the street, "fuck you, you lazy
> piece of shit" I say, angry so I don't feel his pain, happy
> I'm not him and rationalizing his ill fate as our country
> kills babies with low birth rates and single mother
> Medicaid and food stamps for food that ain't nutrient
> for shit and a school system that teaches you a damn,
> the America that creates classes of people working at
> grimy jobs for crooked backs and the Boss's belly with
> police occupying neighborhoods like a goddamn
> military junta, killing some, incarcerating some,
> striking fear into the rest, a country where a young
> man goes to war a proud father and returns a
> daughterless murderer with a psychiatrist and crazy
> pills and nightmares that do the job so the Suits don't
> have to and it's the same country that makes you look
> into the gray doldrums of your miserable existence and
> hate every single thing around you —*

America is at constant war with itself.

XI

Unshaven and sleep-dazed at the breakfast table, Walter stared at his ceramic beige plate and its unflattering display of burnt tofu sausage. His eyes shifted to the right and fixed upon the brownish heap of water-made, microwave oatmeal sitting in the bowl on top of the rough wooden grains. He glanced upward to see a glass of water, and back down at the plate that held his fake brown meat, face numb with stale morning stupor.

He noticed four pills, each a different color and size. There was a long nameless capsule next to a second capsule of red and white, four tiny letters written on the white side. There was a small, round, pallid yellow pill. Then, there was the horse-pill. His eyes burned from staring. He thought about what he should do. He knew he could hide the capsules under his tongue for as long as he had too — it was the other two that were the problem: the pale yellow and the horse-pill would dissolve in his mouth. He reached for his fork, fumbled it lethargically, and then picked it up again. He grabbed his dull butter knife with a little more grace, and began cutting his fake meat.

Low sodium low calorie diet meat. Even so, I like to cut it all up at once and have it all ready, instead a cuttin' off one bite at a time like some kinda lunatic...

Walter finished cutting and stabbed the tines of his fork through two pieces of tofu, eating both. He put his utensils down and reached for his spoon, taking a bite of tasteless oatmeal. He washed it down with water.

He grabbed his fork and went for more tofu. He didn't mind the taste.

It's the goddamn principle of the thing's what it is.

He chewed his fake sausage slowly, holding his fork in the air as if paused in thought. He swallowed his food and reached again for his glass of water. The tofu was awfully dry. He set the glass down on the wood and picked up his spoon, eyeing the oatmeal hesitantly.

The yellow pill ain't so bad, really. Fits right up my nose, just about the color, too...

Walter stared at the big white pill as he swallowed a spoonful of oatmeal.

It's the horse-pill that's the problem. Jesus it's a big'n.

He continued eating his breakfast in a tired trance. He felt like he was thinking, but he wasn't certain. He stared at the last pill as he ate.

She's sitting right across the table. You only get once chance old man.

He chewed in a daze, wide eyes never leaving the big white pill, seeing it and looking through it. His right hand drifted toward it.

"Shit!" Walter exclaimed, recoiling his hand hard and slapping the side of his head like he forgot something, eyes huge and mouth agape. From across the table came a concerned cry:

"What? Dad, what is it?"

Her blue-gray eyes were deep and sensitive, her brow furrowed, hands clutching the side of her paper. Walter rubbed his hand back and forth on the side of his head through his hair as if confused.

"I was supposed to get some stuff around for my group therapy session today," Walter said disappointedly. "We have a bit of a show and tell..."

"No Dad, that's tomorrow," she smiled in knowing relief. "Today you have community engagement at the animal shelter."

"Oh," said Walter in a convincing tone, fading his hand motion into a less noticeable head scratch, "say, you're right." She shook her head, still smiling. She looked backed down at her paper and continued reading, content with the fact that Walter was at least seemingly invested in his therapy.

If anything, they'll think it's my dandruff.

Walter finished his breakfast, gulping the last of his water. She looked up from across the table and noticed his pills were gone. *Today's going to be a good day,* she grinned.

XII

"Are you all right, Walter?"

Dr. C leaned forward in concern. Walter was reclined in his chair, arms limp on the rests, eyes closed, mouth slightly open with tongue draped over bottom teeth, his face sallow and uncomfortable looking. He groaned.

"I feel a little queasy doc, I...I'm just gonna lay here. We can talk I guess, but I don't feel so good."

Dr. C lowered his eyebrows quizzically. "Do you have a fever?"

"I mean, I don't think it's a full blown fever," Walter grumbled weakly, "but I feel hot, that's for sure." He sighed, his body motionless except the rising and falling of his chest. Dr. C frowned, a few wrinkles forming in his balding head. His eyes were stern but touched with worry. "Did you take your pills today?"

"All of 'em," Walter remarked listlessly. Dr. C withheld his excitement.

"Even the big white one?" Dr. C inquired.

"*Especially* the big white one," Walter responded. Dr. C's eyes smiled.

"Well," he began with the proverbial tone of the intuitive

doctor, "I think your body's probably not used to the pills. Yet another reason why it's absolutely essential to stick to your regimen." Walter nodded weakly with closed eyes from his chair.

"You need to take your appropriate medication *every day* to keep this from happening." Walter muttered some sort of affirmation. Dr. C leaned back contentedly on the couch.

"Of course, for the time being, we can increase your meal sizes — put a little more food in your stomach before you take all of that medication." Walter suppressed the giddy tremble in his veins.

"That'd be nice, doc," he said with frail gratitude in his voice.

Dr. C smiled, proud of Walter's compliance and pleased to reward him some. "We can also cut the big white pill in half and have you take part at breakfast and the other part at lunch, so—" Walter bolted up from his chair, a painful hiccup forming in his stomach and pushing forcefully up his chest and throat.

"Excuse me Dr.," Walter moaned through feigned dry heaves, putting his hand up to motion to a concerned Dr. C that he would be fine as he hurried toward the bathroom with sickly determination.

Closing the door behind him, he kneeled beside the toilet and gripped the porcelain. It felt cold in his hands. He spit the two capsule pills from breakfast into the toilet water, dry heaving hard to mask their gentle *kerplunk.* He spit a big pool of saliva in after them, hating the taste they left under his tongue. He then plugged his left nostril and blew hard, shooting the yellow pill out of his nose and into the bowl, making a few more fake vomiting noises before flushing it all down the toilet. He rose to his feet. He reached for the faucet, staring at his tired face in the mirror as he washed his hands.

More food, horse-pills smaller and easier to avoid, everything else down the pipes...

Walter grinned.

And the best part is, I'm right where he thinks I need to be.

Wiping his mouth on his sleeve as he closed the bathroom door, he headed calmly down the hallway and back to his recliner to sit down. He looked weakly at Dr. C.

Tell me I can hope to be normal...

XIII

"Alright, you little bastard," mumbled Walter, stooped over the scruffy pug, fumbling for its leashed collar, "you win." Walter lifted his head and surveyed the surrounding field, his eyes tracing the metal fences. The grounds were empty. He glanced back toward the ennui-gray of the decaying brick animal shelter, a chilly wind passing over his stubbled face. He felt the cold pellet of a tired autumn drizzle on his skin. He turned his eyes toward the flat horizon; its low-lying stratus clouds stretched into a doleful gray infinity. His eyes shifted back to the mangy neck fur of the tired old pug. The dog panted with lazy curiosity, its droopy face half-turned in a lethargic attempt to look over its shoulder to see what Walter was doing, yellow eye straining to see past its jowls. Walter reached again for the link between leash and collar; the metal slipped in his stiff, cold hands. The dog lolled his head back to look excitedly at Walter, rolling and craning its neck without turning its body, breathing hard over its drooling tongue. Walter gripped the icy metal of the collar and leash hard in each cold, unmoving hand, refusing to let either slip again. He dug his thumb into the rusty catching latch of the leash, pulling down the crude button until it opened the hook. Now, all he had to do was hold his stiff hands in position and move his left arm downward until the link of the collar pulled free from the hook of the leash. He struggled for a while. It was nearly impossible to unhook a leash without the luxury of supple joints or ligaments.

The latch impressed into the skin of his thumb and made a small indentation in the bone. Tremors shot through his forearms and into his locked wrists, his shaky hands scratching the hook and link together in a series of small metallic squinks. His whole body tightened as he concentrated on one tiny, nimble maneuver.

Come on you little fucker, come on...

Sweat formed on Walter's forehead. It felt strange in the late October chill.

Come on, damnit, come on...

Walter moved the hook and link around in clumsy jerks, his knuckles scraping the brittle unwashed fur of the pug.

COME ON!

The old pug lowered its left shoulder and rolled its back and neck toward the ground. "You little bastard!" Walter started to say, "I was just about to get—" He felt the satisfying slip of the hook leaving the chain of the collar. He looked down to find himself clutching the metal of the leash, its nylon rope hanging from his palm in the wind and licking the blades of dying autumn grass. He cast his gaze toward the pug. It turned to face Walter, giving him a sly drooling grin.

"Well I'll be," Walter mused happily, "I guess I couldn't do all the work for ya."

He reached down and nuzzled the dog's furry head. The pug closed his eyes and raised his head toward the pleasure of the scratching. It was a long time before Walter withdrew.

"Say," Walter said, stooped over and speaking directly to the dog. "How'd you like to bust on outta here?" The pug cocked his head in interest, looking every bit the caricature of the curious dog. Walter extended his arms to scoop up the aging pug, figuring it might be too old to make it across the grounds.

"WAIT."

Walter recoiled in horror, staring at the pug's smiling Buddha-body in the brown grass. He couldn't remember if he took his pills or not, or which choice let him talk to dogs.

"I need to walk the yard myself," Walter heard the dog say. It turned and walked away, leaving him standing in the gray. The dog dawdled across the grounds, Walter watching

its wrinkled frame struggle through the grass underneath the bleak and overcast sky. It headed for the fence.

The world outside the shelter's too big for a pug — he'll never make it...

"What about the fence — the other side?" Walter worried through the wind. The pug kept plodding on. From over its furry shoulder Walter heard the grumbled response:

"I'll deal with it when I get there."

....

I can't believe he let that fucking dog loose. She sat at the kitchen table, fuming over Walter's Tuesday evening antics, envisioning the burly scrubbed male vets striding across the animal shelter's wide grounds, Walter standing in the windy yard, babbling to himself as the pug receded into the horizon. *And when they reach him, winded and out of breath, what does he say?* she steamed. *What does he say? He says, "He told me to do it." The fucking dog! Of course he told you to do it. And of course they ask, "Well, how Walter?" And he says, "With words, you fags."*

Her cheeks burned in humiliation. They'd be lucky if the animal shelter allowed Walter to return. She figured she should look up other charities to satisfy the community engagement component of Walter's therapy. She sighed, alone and worried in thought. After some time, she rose and left the kitchen, her eyes falling upon a disheveled Walter huddled forward in his corner armchair. She was usually able to contextualize his actions in relation to his trauma, but this...

She shook her head as she walked through the crowded living room for the front door, opening it quietly but closing it hard behind her, leaving Walter clutching his sepia faded photograph in the patient quiet of his Wednesday group therapy session.

It was his turn to share. He could hear his thoughts call from his brain and into his ears, down into his throat, but the room was silent. Time dilated into heavy, crushing moments. He wished the floor would swallow him, but the anticipation of his inevitable words kept him anchored in his huddled stare. He searched the photograph for answers. He saw his young, smiling face with full brown hair neat and slightly combed over, standing tall and lean with rake in hand, its teeth buried under a small layer of sepia tone maples. Next to him, his three-year-old daughter burst forth from a pile, her small hands outstretched as the leaves broke and swirled about her, her smile frozen forever in the autumnal tornado. Walter studied the picture further, making out the beautiful figure of his wife's shadow across the dead maple leaves as she snapped the photo.

"She took this."

Walter's voice broke the silence of the room. The group tilted their heads and smiled in synched sadness. His fingertips grew anxious and sweaty from grasping the sides of the photograph. He didn't want to talk anymore, but knew he had to.

"She took this of me and Evee, right before she died..." Walter trailed off, his throat becoming smaller. The surrounding heaviness was stifling. He felt dumb for being so vulnerable. He stared hard at the picture, hoping everything around him would dissolve. The others watched him with an empathetic patience. He hated them for it.

....After two minutes and forty seconds of silence, Dr. C finally spoke.

"Walter," he began passionately, "thank you so much for sharing." The others nodded with sad eyes. Dr. C gave a subtle nod to Robert. Robert was waiting for it through his commiseration. He offered a considerate pause before beginning.

"Before my condition, my sons and I used to go sailing..." Walter thought about his daughter and his dead wife and how young he used to look, the background noise of Robert's happy droning just reaching his ears over the loud sound of his own quiet stare.

....

Throughout the next morning and into the afternoon, Walter felt ashamed for opening up as much as he did during his group therapy session. But at precisely 3:08 pm, he felt downright stupid. It was then — standing in the cold cement halls of echoing yelps and barks and animal urine, dogs hurtling their paws against cages and cats scurrying — Walter saw a tall, burly male vet walk out of the abyss of the animal shelter holding a leash, the old pug trotting sluggishly alongside.

"There you are, Walter," he smiled as he handed Walter the leash. "Please be more careful this time." Walter thought he saw the man wink as he disappeared around the corner.

He looked down at the old pug. The dog cocked its head curiously as if to say, "*Well?*"

Walter headed for the exit, the dog scampering behind. The door was reminiscent of prison. He pushed it open, fresh autumn air rescuing his lungs from the warmth of stale pee and animal refuse. He walked across the grounds, trying not to look at the dog. He didn't know what to say.

From across the grounds Walter spotted a black figure. It was near the place where he had unleashed the pug the previous Tuesday. He walked over to it. It was a man with slick black hair, sunglasses, suit and tie. He said something in

94

an earpiece as Walter approached, then nodded hello. Walter stopped and looked down at the old pug.

"Well old man, I guess freedom's a continuum," the dog shrugged.

???

   ???

    ...

     ....Walter detected the smell of French onion, and he knew he was daydreaming. The image of his dream swirled and frothed until it faded into the bubbling broth of reality at the soup kitchen — standing over a steaming pot of questions and stirring emptily, wondering if the old pug was alright.

"Hey old man, I'm fucking starving!"

A ratty, twenty-something delinquent with a Slipknot beanie snapped Walter's reverie.

This was his Thursday afternoon.

Walter grumbled as he stirred the soup with the ladle, watching the broth swirl and boil and change colors.

"Fucking pillhead."

He scooped up the broth and poured it into the bowl, passing it to the young man with a forced smile. The delinquent took it without thanking him and cowered in the corner, scarfing it down before running up the steps from the church basement.

Walter gritted his teeth. He hated his new community engagement. He thought about the old pug, wondering if it'd traded its new freedom for convenience.

Least I won't have to do this much longer...

XIV

Walter headed for the door, slipping his worn brown
shoes over his veiny white feet, his pajama bottoms stopping
short at the ankle. He wore a white t-shirt and no hat, his
crazy gray hair unwashed and styled by his pillow — hardly
ready for the cold outdoors of a late October flurry. He
twisted the knob and pushed open the screen. He smiled as
he walked down the steps and began the long, slow, Friday
morning shuffle across his dreary snow-drizzled patch of
Northeast Indiana, heading for the mailbox.

The cold bit his ears and tossed his hair. He lowered his
face and shoulder to the wind, determined to reach the
mailbox, forever plodding through the bitterness of the
flurry. He finally felt the frosty metal of the old mailbox in his
hands, leaning on it for support while sliding his right hand
toward its face to pull the latch. He opened its shoot and
stooped over to peer inside its shadowed mouth. He reached
inside, removing one wadded envelope after another,
crumpling the junk mail and tossing it carelessly to the
ground.

There it is.

There was one envelope left, the one Walter wanted. And though he knew the exact contents of the envelope every time, it was still so exciting.

Every American gets excited over money.

Walter pulled out a letter from the federal government. He inspected it warily — feeling paranoid, as was his custom — before shrugging and tearing it open. It was his benefits check. Or, as he liked to say:

My check from the government for being crazy.

It was all there, Walter's monthly stipend. He counted it again and again, doing mental calculations to double check. He felt ironic in the cold, clinging desperate to a piece of paper claiming it paid him enough for his service to his country. He felt even worse about his excitement over receiving such a miniscule sum.

Government thinks they're clever, goddamn giving me peanuts for my soul, thinking I don't know. There ain't enough money in this world to take away what I saw, to undo what I done...

Walter trudged across the dead grass and snow of his desolate yard. He opened the front door to a concerned daughter standing in the middle of the threshold. He handed her his check, grumbling in submission. Because Walter was deemed unfit to take care of himself, she budgeted his finances — though he did stash some money in a shoebox in his closet. Walter plopped into his living room chair, muttering to himself.

"Sell my soul to the devil and my loot gets taxed by an angel."

"Dad, I can buy that coffee you like," she offered from near the door.

"That's ok, pumkin," he sighed. "You do whatever you want. You always know how to take care of me."

She tried not to cry through her smile. He ignored her teary eyes and obvious sniffles, slightly annoyed as he reached for the TV remote.

Thank God I got all that beer in my closet.

....

There were fewer beers than Walter remembered. He fished through the rummage and rattle of empty cans, his hand finding a full pilsner and wrapping his stiff fingers around the smoothness of the aluminum. He pulled it through the top layer of refuse and toward his shirt, dusting off the wide mouth before peeling back the pull tab and placing everything in its appropriate pile. Walter took a slug of the warm golden beer, enjoying the crispy burn down his throat and into his stomach. He leaned against the soft decay of the closet wall, sipping his beer and thinking.

Lotta empty beer cans, about time I do something with those.

Walter examined the can. He admired its simple artwork before taking another drink. He lowered his beer and scanned the aluminum for the cuts he would make. He needed to start right away. Walter crinkled his can some as he threw his head back and chugged the rest of the beer, his eyes watering as he wiped his mouth with a flannel sleeve.

Ain't got time to waste! Now where's them scissors...?

Walter tossed the beer can, rifling through the junk for a pair of scissors. He had twenty-four years' worth of aluminum to cut. He didn't have much time.

XV

—*Garcia from the stretch now, runner on first, one man out, the count 1-2. Checks over his shoulder before the delivery...wow, really put some heat into that one but it's low and away and the count is 2-2. I tell you he's really been an asset for Chicago.*

—*No doubt about that, Pat. Cincinnati's struggled up to bat against him, a ball club that had one of the highest batting averages this regular season.*

—*Right Don, safe to say that's what probably got them through October, but today we've gotta classic pitcher's duel on our hands, a real battle of the wills as Garcia nods to Bennet behind the plate and leans back to gather himself before the pitch, Anderson on first base with a modest lead, Garcia checks the runner and fires...*

The images of the baseball game reflected through Walter's gray irises, kindling his pupil and fading into his bloodshot corneas. TV glow flashed against the living room blinds, setting the familiar scene of an American evening — Walter and his neighbors all sitting motionless in the blue radiance.

—Myyy goodness, the fans not too happy about that one, called ball on the outside corner of the plate and I tell you that hadt've just missed by an inch. Garcia's really working the zone and I think he deserved that one.

—I think you're right Pat. Let's look at the replay on our strike zone cam...

—Ooo, yep.

—[Chuckling]

—He'll have to shake it off. He walks to the mound and digs into the rubber, leaning forward to take the signal from Bennett, shakes his head, agrees, sets, checking the runner, looks back to the plate, the 3-2 pitch...Garcia turns and whips it to first base and oh! Anderson just under the tag! Crowd thought he had him.

—He's been doing a good job of keepin' him honest over there, Anderson being known to swipe his share of bases, got on with a bunt, speed obviously his strong suit.

—Garcia back in the stretch, sets, checks Anderson, waits, still looking over his shoulder, Hoffman at first base holding him on, Garcia looks back toward the plate, Kullinger gripping his bat, ready for the 3-2...

She wandered into the room, frowning at Walter's fixation and the loud volume of the television — but inwardly she was relieved. If sitting sedentary in front of the TV stopped the madness then that was fine with her. She was running out of energy, and his behavior was increasingly harder to manage. Plus, she couldn't shake the notion that he was up to something.

"Can you turn that down, Dad, please?"

—*Fouls it off and Kullinger's hanging in there! This is shaping up to be a pretty good at-bat!*

Walter didn't move. He said nothing, leaving her an unacknowledged TV-glow silhouette in the entryway. She sighed, waiting a few seconds for a response she knew wasn't coming before sitting down on the couch. She never took her eyes off of him. He sat in his blue shadowed stupor, dazed but still watching the television with vigilance, arms at the side of his chair, legs extended on the footrest, mouth open slightly, still.

—*Garcia digs in, nods to Bennet behind the plate.*

"Dad?"

—*Anderson takes his lead.*

"Dad."

—*Garcia sets.*

"DAD."

Walter reached for the remote and turned up the volume, her disgusted huff drowning in the blare of TV and baseball.

—FOULS IT AWAY TO STAY ALIVE! [CROWD ROARS].

"TURN THAT DOWN!" she yelled, exasperated.

"You didn't have to come in here," Walter retorted coldly. She glared at him in the changing television light for a few seconds before dropping her eyes to the floor. She listened to the sounds of the baseball game: the commentators, the raucous murmur of the crowd, the dull snap of the catcher's glove, the hometown organ playing tunes just audible through the televised coverage. The defense went to offense went to defense. Innings passed with her staring at the floor, burning, Walter immobile in the shadow of the TV. She raised her eyes to look at him again. The way the television light fell on him made him look twisted and dark. For a moment, she didn't know who he was.

"Dad?" her voice trembled some, breaking the silence.

"Hnnh?" Walter grunted without moving. She measured her words carefully. She wasn't feeling very good and didn't want to upset him. She averted her gaze, choosing to stare emptily at the TV for a while.

"Dad," she began again, turning to look at Walter. "When you're in your room," she faltered, unsure of how to ask. "When you're in your room, well, today I heard... " He continued staring into the TV.

"What are you up to?" she finally blurted out.

Walter didn't look at her.

"What am *I* up to? What exactly are *you* up to?" he growled.

She recoiled, looking at Walter with pain in her eyes, stammering, "I, I — what do you mean?"

Walter reached for the remote and pressed the mute button, hateful eyes never leaving the television.

"Why are you always over here?" he demanded.

She gasped. "Because I, I—"

"What are you always reading?

Where do you go after you drop me off?

What do you do during my therapy sessions?

What do you and the doc talk about?

Matter of fact, what the fuck do *you* do when I'm in my room?"

She stared blankly at Walter, hurt. A tear formed in her eye as she watched him scowl at the television. She felt like she was failing, and she didn't know what to say. In the last ten days, Walter had become even more paranoid and distrustful than usual. She hoped it would all end after the 24th, the anniversary of his wife's death. Until then, he would need increasing support, and more monitoring.

She continued watching him through the light and shadow of the flickering TV. *He needs more pills, really,* she thought. Dr. C was convinced that Walter was taking the right amount — and actually taking them. She sighed.

Walter turned the volume back up. The television roared with the sounds of nighttime Americana, an October Classic in the Midwest.

—PERFECT AUTUMN NIGHT FOR THIS SERIES, PAT.
—AND WHATTA NIGHT IT'S BEEN, DON. IF YOU'RE JUST NOW JOINING US AT HOME, IT'S BEEN A DEFENSIVE SHOWDOWN AS WE HEAD INTO THE EIGHTH INNING, BOTH TEAMS SCORELESS, CASPER TRYING TO GET THINGS SHAKING FOR CHICAGO. NO SIGNAL FROM THIRD BASE AS HE DIGS INTO THE BOX, LOOKING AT SOUTHPAW RIVERA ON THE MOUND, TALL AND LANKY HURLER UP THERE.
—AND DOES THIS KID REACH BACK AND FIRE, PAT.
—HE SURE DOES, DON. RIVERA FROM THE WINDUP, CATCHES THE SIGNAL FROM BEHIND THE PLATE, BARING DOWN ON CASPER, CASPER GLARING BACK.
—YOU CAN REALLY FEEL THAT COLD WIND BLOW HERE IN CHICAGO.

....

She came to the room later. Walter lay reclined in his tattered green armchair, the footrest extended and his legs straight, a frayed and faded quilt draped around his legs, his head tipped back and his mouth open, drool forming at the corner of his mouth, the television blasting. *He's asleep.* She smiled.

She tiptoed across the living room, reaching slowly for the remote on Walter's armrest. His arm was touching the remote, and she had to remove it carefully to keep him from stirring. Once she accomplished this, she turned quietly and pressed the off-button. Silence cut the last loud echo of the television. She soundlessly placed the remote back down next to Walter and receded to her usual spot on the couch, picking her reading up from the living room floor and getting to work.

The living room was quiet. She wasn't sure how much time had passed. She looked up at Walter, his black socks stretched thin over his pointed toes, frayed quilt over his thighs, silent and motionless at the edge of the footrest. His evening pills sat dusty on the sill next to a half-drunk glass of water. She turned back to her latest report, not hearing the countless ticks of the antique clock ushering the passing evening.

The sudden grind of the footrest snapping into place under the chair warned her to put down her reading. Walter threw out his crooked arms as he launched from the recliner, scurrying to the door in a clumsy panic, scrambling for the porch light switch on the outdated vinyl wall. "*THE SUITS!*" he cried in ecstatic terror. "*THE SUITS!*" He tore the door open, stumbling into the yellow light of his front yard.

"There they go!"

She was already at the threshold of the door, looking into the cold October night. Breeze rustled the leaves and flitted through the tips of buried grass, the blades fading into their winter colors. Walter raved in the driveway, cursing the moon.

"YOU BASTARDS! I FUCKING SEE YOU!"

Walter's words shook the night. Somewhere in the quiet neighborhood, worried lights flickered on. There was the distant sound of dogs barking. She watched his tragic figure — bent, twisted, screaming obscenities into the darkness.

At first, she was sad as she watched him shake his bony knuckles in rage. Then, she thought about all the places those hands had been, and started laughing.

"I KNOW YOU'RE OUT THERE!" bellowed Walter.

She turned her back, laughing into the front door, fumbling for the knob. She kept giggling as she opened the door, stumbling inside to hide her less than sympathetic response.

YOU FUCKING CANDYASS PIECES OF SHIT!"

She burst out laughing, closing the door behind her to welcome the warmth of the living room. Today, she was over it. Tomorrow, things wouldn't be so funny.

Frankly, things wouldn't be funny at all.

She reached in her pocket for her phone, stifling her laughter and getting serious. She needed to report everything to Dr. C.

XVI

Walter rounded the corner, dreading his Monday morning one-on-one therapy session with Dr. C. He entered his living room, muttering to himself. When he looked up, he was even angrier than he anticipated. There was Dr. C in his usual spot, smiling confidently at Walter. But Walter was surprised to see a worried-eyed daughter, his team of nurses (who typically didn't arrive until 10:00), and even the liaison who worked to place Walter at first the animal shelter and now the soup kitchen. And he was exceptionally mortified to see Robert, group therapy exemplar, warm smile barely concealing his concern.

Walter said "Hello," with cold, unhappy surprise. Everyone in the room watched as he sauntered over to his chair without making any eye contact, turned, and plopped down into it, slouching. He looked up to meet their stares, responding with a wry smirk.

"Walter," began Dr. C, "it's been brought to my attention that you've been — how should I say this — acting out lately." He tilted his head to Walter, "Care to explain?"

"Yes, doc," said Walter absently. Figuring he was getting lectured, he had already checked out. He waited for Dr. C to speak again. Dr. C raised his eyebrows as a provocation for Walter. Walter wasn't paying attention. He was staring blankly, inside his head, thinking about his dream.

I'm walking through the fear and the terror, the death, only now I can see the faces of the crowd. I'm in a village somewhere, their dusty faces are caked with sadness; I know they're farmers. They're skinny, and I can tell they don't have much food. Their dead eyes follow me as I walk towards the center. I don't look at them, but I see grandmothers without shoes and teeth, wearing war-torn cloth, holding their hands out to me, their palms turned to the sky for mercy. I keep my eyes straight, but I see dark-haired mothers in dirty scarves, beautiful eyes and strong faces, stifling cries, wrapping their children in their rags to shield them from the horror. And I see the motherless children, ragamuffin and watching me with nothing in their eyes. I keep my eyes fixed on the rebel daughter. She's in front on her bony little girl knees, staring at me, and I want to look beyond her at the men my troop can blame for this to sleep at night but I feel the horrid small gasp of the crowd as I reach into my holster and draw out my pistol, angry and quick, and now I'm holding it to her forehead. I can feel their desperate eyes on my back. I feel scared, but I know I'm in control. I press the barrel into her forehead and it gives a little. I see every little detail and contour and the lines and colors of her little eyes, and I grit my teeth. Right before I pull

*the trigger I hear a desperate voice from the darkness. It
makes me jump a little, and I do it. I blow her brains out. And
her blood and the contents of her skull splatter all over me, and
it's all so real this time. And I drop my gun and look at my
hands, and there's blood all over them. Somebody — one of the
troops — comes up to me, reaches out his hand to reassure me.*

"She had brown hair," I say to the dirt. "And bl—"

I wake up.

"Walter, care to explain?" Dr. C repeated. Reality was the
faint tug of nausea, a full living room and an expectant Dr. C.
Walter wondered if they had seen his thoughts, the new
details of his dream. He hoped they hadn't. He searched the
faces of everyone in the room. Their sad-eyed concern made
him angry.

They come into my living room, he thought, his eyes tracing a
muddy trail of footprints across the beige carpet, *plop right
down on my furniture...* he saw the trail stop at a pair of old
boots, *then they all lean in like a goddamn family at an
intervention and tell me how to think and act and feel —*

Walter traced the boots upward, stopping at Robert's
worried frown.

AND THEY DON'T TAKE THEIR FUCKING SHOES OFF.

He scowled at Robert. Then he shifted his eyes from face to face, from shoe to shoe. Every last shoe was caked in October mud. A heaviness formed in his periphery and sucked into his chest, a burden resting in his heart. He felt the slow wane of time and its string of short, passing moments. Face — shoe — face — shoe — face — shoe — shoe — mud — dirt — dirt — dirt: he cast paranoid looks at the door, his anxiety mounting, the tick-tock of the clock the only sound in the room. Walter waited, a thousand thoughts hurtling themselves against the inside of his body. He couldn't decide which thoughts were important, which ones were appropriate, and which ones would make him too vulnerable. Dr. C raised his eyebrows again, expecting an answer. Walter thought about how he felt towards each individual in the room, and what he wanted to say. He hated all of them.

"Walter, can you share with us whatever's on your mind?" inquired Dr. C. Walter grinned.

Whatever's on my mind?

"I only have one thing to say," Walter began coolly, voice rising. His audience was at full attention.

"And that's take your GODDAMN SHOES OFF AT THE FUCKING DOOR YOU INCONSIDERATE PIECES OF SHIT!"

Dr. C recoiled. The nurses gasped. Robert cast a painful look to the floor, shaking his head in disappointment. Walter smiled.

"Walter," sighed Dr. C., "I know you don't trust us. But we are here to help."

Help? Walter stifled a sardonic laugh.

"We're all here to support you, Dad."

Walter found it humorous, how seriously everyone took their roles. He looked at the community engagement liaison, wondering what he could possibly be thinking: *Over there, looking concerned — I barely even know the fucker.* Walter chuckled inside his head. *He doesn't give a shit, and neither do I.* He turned, noticing Robert shifting in his seat. *Oh,* he thought in a pompous tone, *looks like our buddy Robert has something to say!*

"Walter," Robert began, "we've known each other for a long time now." The words sounded strange to Walter. Sure, he had been in group therapy with Robert for nearly twenty-five years, but he never would have said it involved *knowing* Robert. "I just want you to be happy, old friend." A tear slid down Robert's face. "And I, for one, will do whatever it takes." He started crying. Walter felt embarrassed.

So cliché. Like a goddamn movie.

"We're *all* willing to do whatever it takes, Walter," reassured Dr. C. The room was full of tragic nods and sure eyes. "And that's why we're here today, because we've been failing you."

No shit.

"We haven't been trying hard enough," Dr. C sighed with disappointment.

Wait, what?

"Dad, we've all been talking." She looked at Walter's glowering eyes, stuttering a little as she continued, "A-and we think it'd be best if we could offer you more support."

MORE?

Walter looked toward the community engagement liaison with a bitter smile, thinking *surely you can't agree with this you indifferent bastard...*The man stared back at him, looking sympathetic. Walter tried the nurses, knowing they wouldn't want more of his smart-ass remarks and noncompliant behaviors. Their eyes drowned him in pity. Walter squirmed some in his seat. "More of what?"

"More time, more activities, more therapy — more everything," remarked Dr. C. Walter's heart sank. "That's what you need. And we need to work harder to give that to you." The crowd nodded dolefully. They were there to support him.

"I'm fine doc, really." Walter looked to each face with desperate appeal. Their sad eyes looked back. Walter couldn't convince them of anything.

"Dad..." She reached her hand out toward Walter, her blue-gray eyes despondent and willing, "you are not well. You know I love you, but you are not okay right now and, and..." she choked on the tearful lump in her throat, closed her eyes hard and shook her head, crying.

Jesus H.

"So," began Dr. C definitively, but with caution, "starting today, we will have a team meeting *every morning* at 8:00am. The team is all right here." Dr. C swept his hand across the room. Walter gulped, suppressing his reaction. He didn't know if he was angry or anxious or humiliated. He was no more than the burning in his gut, the heaviness in his chest. "We'll begin with our team meeting at 8:00, sharing our challenges and celebrations with one another until our 9:00 therapy session...." Dr. C's voice faded into white noise over the sound of Walter's thoughts getting louder and louder.

These motherfuckers.

Walter looked around the room, through the drone of Dr. C's new regimen of care and support. His eyes scanned each face. Robert was genuinely upset. It made Walter sick. His nurses were sympathetic and worried, and it made him feel small. Walter was comforted by the superficiality of the one he didn't really know, but it didn't compensate for the outrage he felt towards this stranger in his house attempting to care.

I can't stand these bastards and their mock concern, showing me the way to a better life. I can't stand the game, I just can't stand the game.

Dr. C looked upon Walter with professional courtesy. He had just finished speaking. Walter knew it was his turn. He shook his head and held out his hands, beginning to mouth his words, the air pressing up from his throat harder and harder to form them. He laughed, shaking his head with contempt and looking to the floor. The others looked at him curiously.

I just can't stand the game, the clichés, taking turns playing roles, the way they all wait for me to say what I have to say like they care but they just yield the floor to me for a second so they can go on with the decision they've already made, teary-eyed and worried...

"Well, Walter, what do you think? This is about you, and we need you to be on board."

You need me to be on board so you can cover all your bases like a goddamn diplomat. Christ, I can't stand the song and dance. I just can't fucking stand the game.

"Dad...?"

"Sure," I hear myself say as I look up, going along with their plan. They all smile and sort of lean back in relief, exchanging satisfied looks. Alone in the chair, I feel vulnerable — but then she floats towards me with tears in her eyes, arms outstretched, overwhelmed with my half-ass commitment to happiness. And I'm starting to think I love her when I feel Robert's strong arms and the gentle reassuring hand of the doc on my shoulder, and before I know it we're all pulling it in for a team hug...stop touching me goddamnit.

Walter grimaced quietly in the group's embrace. He had them right where he wanted them.

XVII

It was Sunday, and she was supposed to be supervising him; Walter's room was locked, as usual. She stood puzzled outside the door, muffled sounds of whirring gears floating from the bedroom and stopping short in the hallway. She pressed her ear to the o ak. Around the corner of the shambled closet, across the old man's bedroom, through the grains of oak and trembling lightly to her ear — the faint grinding din of what sounded like an overworked blender. She scrunched her face, listening, trying to place the sound. The grinding was relatively consistent though it would sporadically catch and push with a forceful whine, the tambour of the desperate cogs barely audible, the blender teeth stuck grinding something too big. A little scuffle — the sounds of Walter adjusting something in his closet — and the high whir of the gears could be heard once more. She kept her ear to the door, wondering what he could be doing and feeling somewhat unsettled. She listened so long that she could hear the nuances of what she had thought to be a blended unison; over the general buzz rose the high hum of a second machine. She waited patiently, anticipating the grinding stop-and-go pattern of the gears. The machines caught, pushed, stopped — a brief fumbling — and they started again, but this time out of synch. There were three different frequencies, maybe four. She frowned at the thought of Walter having three or four secrets. She concentrated harder through the door. *What's he doing in there?* she thought.

Inside the closet, Walter wiped the sweat from his brow with his forearm, careful not to spill or even touch his concoction. He emptied the contents of two of the coffee grinders into a safe container, the other two still grinding on top of the only level part of the collapsing shelf. He figured he had about twenty-four minutes before the usual knock on his door. He nodded his head, self-affirming and a little drunk from finishing the last of his hidden beer.

This just might work....

She listened intently, guessing that Walter had three or four blenders in his room — but why? She kept her ear pressed to the door, hoping it would tell her what to do.

GSZZHH...
   Zzzzzzzzzzz
      zzzzzzzzz
         zzzz...zzzt. zzt.
            mmmzt. mmmzt.
               mmmmm...

The motor stopped. She was listening so hard for sound that she didn't hear the silence. Without making any noise, Walter cleaned up and carefully closed the closet door behind him, then headed for the hallway. She was surprised by his soft and sudden footsteps just inside the door. She fumbled at the threshold, trying to mitigate the sound of her surprise while edging away.

A sudden crash against the bedroom door made her jump, and she let out a short scream. She covered her mouth and took a step back, eyeing the door with concern. The knob spun with slow curiosity but turned to a violent shake before Walter ripped open the heavy oaken door with a bang, stumbling into the light of the hallway. He reoriented himself then tripped backwards, reaching for the wall behind him for balance. He caught himself, dusted off, and straightened up, drunken eyes still squinting in the light. She cocked her head in a surprised frown, trying her best to look as though she had just approached the door.

Walter hiccupped.

It was her ticket: if she could call him out first, her eavesdropping would be forgotten. She started to open her mouth—

"What are you doing?" they said simultaneously. Walter smirked. He'd been waiting. She sighed, trying not to smile, not even a little bit. She opted for rolling her eyes.

"Aw, c'mon pumkin," slurred Walter, stumbling forth to put his arm around her. She glanced sideways through his half hug.

"Dad," she began, "Have you been—"

"Gotta go," he hollered over his shoulder as he broke away, hurrying toward the living room, "Garcia's pitchin' tonight; need ta make sure I get a good seat." He cackled at his own joke. She shook her head in dismay. If he kept acting this way, she would have to confer with Dr. C. If he kept acting this way, there would need to be a new course of action. There would need to be more.

Surely he wasn't drunk, she lied to herself.

XVIII

Thank God that's over.

Walter brushed his shoulders off. He felt unclean. He never
wanted to be anywhere near a group hug ever again.

Fucking rats' nest.

He could hear the sounds of jackets and nylon, handshakes
and sincere words, mudcaked footsteps and the opening and
closing of the front door as he receded down the hallway. His
first "team therapy" session was wrapping up. He walked
into his bedroom, closing the door on the fading scene
behind him.

He sat down on the edge of his bed and stared at the
wall. The paint was beginning to peel. Monday morning
sunlight fell weakly on the cracks. Walter studied the
chips — their shapes and size, the ruggedness of their
edges — and the way the faint shadows fell in between them.
Some made images, others were suggestions. They all ran
together as Walter bore his eyes into the cream-stained
walls.

She was only a little girl. Eleven years old to be exact.

Walter saw it all unfold before him, a distant memory on a faded wall. He could see himself thirty years younger, healthier, and happier. The pain in his eyes had grown some, but he was altogether doing fine. He had his daughter, and they were content.

Before the war.

He was wearing his service uniform, trying not to look at the sadness in her eyes as she approached the car. She had her mother's eyes. Some days, it was just too much.

Walter stared across the dash and through the windshield as she opened the passenger door, greeting her with a sad smile. "Hi Dad!" she exclaimed, climbing in. Her enthusiasm tugged a chord in Walter's heart. She knew she wouldn't see him for some time, but she chose to celebrate their final moments together rather than color them melancholy, to be stronger than fear. This was his little Evee.

She reached for the seatbelt and pulled it over her puffy nylon jacket. Walter could hear her smile and the sounds of her settling in. She let her palms fall to her knees as if to say, "Well!", waiting for any sort of cue from her father. His eyes were locked on the nothingness beyond the windshield.

"Dad," she began, smiling sheepishly. Walter shook off

his trance and turned toward her.

"Yes pumkin?" His eyes were gray and hurt.

"Do you wanna maybe start the car?" she grinned. Walter glanced up at the rearview mirror, seeing a fleet of antsy minivans and sedans full of soccer moms and dads queuing behind him.

"Oh, right," he said absentmindedly, reaching to turn the key in the ignition. The car jumped forward. Walter gassed it to show the other parents that he cared about hurrying like everyone else. They wound through the school lot, stopping at the stop sign before accelerating to join the contiguous neighborhood road. Walter gripped the steering wheel, hands at a perfect 10 and 2, his eyes back to their zoned stare through the windshield. Evee studied the side of his face with a curious smile. She admired his classic jaw and clean shave, his somber eyes. She liked his uniform, but thought it made him look too constrained; she could see his lean muscles and bones poking out against the fabric. She knew her dad was strong, but a nagging doubt overshadowed by childhood adulation told her in dying whispers that he was all too vulnerable. She shook her head, giggling at his solemnity to shed her uncertainty. Walter glanced downward at her, smiling nervously. He figured he should slow down to make the moment last. They drove in silence.

Is this how the memory will go? Sad and quiet?

Walter checked the mirror, shifted his eyes toward his daughter, then back to the road. He didn't feel like talking but favored it over regret. Even so, it all felt so forced. He was going to war, and nobody knew when he would come back. There was nothing he could say to change that. He felt heavy, boxed in; he was nothing more than a small, insecure version of himself trapped in a moment, the last moment. He couldn't wait for it all to be over; and yet, he felt time eluding him and hated the familiar street signs for telling him so. If he could just slow down: the car, little Evee, the war. It all just needed to slow down.

Life waits for no one.

Walter looked into the mirror. There was a line of cars behind him. He checked his speedometer, seeing it read 10mph less than the limit. He jumped a little, gassing the vehicle before taking an abrupt left turn, his daughter smiling out the window at the scene rushing past. She knew where they were going.

....

The tires rolled to a slow stop upon the uncut September grass, the sigh of the dying engine echoing underneath the metal of the hood and fading throughout the car. Evee looked up through the window at the sunlit canopy of the big maple, its summer green beginning its gradual turn to auburn. She heard the car door open and the rustling of leaves, her father coming into view through the glass as he drifted towards the tree. He stopped a few feet from where she sat in the passenger seat, putting his hands in his pockets and gazing upwards. She watched him with a contemplative half-smile for a few seconds before getting out and walking towards him, looking up at the tree when she reached his side.

They stood silently, gazing upwards with bent necks, eyes full of leaves. Walter looked stoic. His daughter glanced sideways, unable to see the mind racing tumult underneath his squinting, weathered face.

Right here, last autumn with Mom, the colors and the leaves and the slow dying maple.

His stare never broke. He thought of all the perfect things to say and how none of them were true.

"You don't have to say anything, Dad."

Walter looked down at his daughter in surprise. He started to stutter, but her loving smile dissolved his stammering words, making him feel warm. He put his arm around her and held her close.

....

The low rumble of the car engine as it sat in idle in front of her grandparents' home; Evee sitting, antsy; Walter looking through the windshield, unwilling to start the goodbye: this was his last memory. Time passed. Walter couldn't distinguish seconds from hours from minutes. His stomach rose high into his chest and he looked straight ahead at nothing. He could hear her soft squirm in the passenger seat.

"Evee," he found himself saying in a reserved, didactic tone, "I don't want to leave you, but sometimes a man has to do what's right." He turned to her. She was surprised at how proud and unwavering he looked. So was he. "And sometimes doing what's right involves making sacrifices. But making sacrifices is what this country's always been about, and I for one will do what I can to protect freedom, to serve God and country. And that means I have to make a sacrifice, pumkin. We all have to make a sacrifice..." Walter faltered, then stopped. He tried his best to look heroic.

"There are little girls, just like you, all over the world. They're not free. They need the USA, a country made of fine people like you and me." Walter looked past his daughter, self-importance in his face but remorse in his chest. He couldn't really see her, and he didn't want to. It would be too painful.

"Sure, Dad," she smiled, kissing him on the cheek as she moved to unbuckle her seatbelt. She got out of the car and opened the rear passenger door to grab her things. She turned toward her grandparents' home. It was her home for now. Maybe her father wouldn't even come back at all.

"Evee," Walter called through the passenger window, "I promise I'll be back soon." She stared at him with her blue-gray eyes, seeing through his planned phrases.

"I love you, Evee," he said.

She was glad to hear the truth at last.

XIX

Who the hell are they?

There were two new male nurses in Walter's 10:00am goal-setting session. They sat close to one another and were of similar build; both also had black hair and early thirties professionalism etched into their faces. They wore scrubs like the other nurses.

The head nurse was saying something. Walter wasn't listening.

I think I've seen these two before...

He alternated between hard scrupulous stares and darting eyes, trying to study their faces without looking obvious. It was noticeable. The nurses just smiled.

"Are you ready, Walter?" he heard someone say. He stared blankly. "Ok, why don't we start by setting our goals? Should we work on positive eye contact this week?"

He nodded from time to time.

"....constructive ways to express our feelings?"

His body language was respectful.

"....reward for every day you adhere to your regimen?"

When it was his turn to speak, he responded appropriately.

"....contributing two positive remarks during each group therapy session?"

Walter appeared to be listening.

"....build trust with your teammates?"

He wasn't.

He couldn't stop thinking about the new nurses. He was sure he knew them from somewhere. He shot them quick glances between giving positive eye contact to whoever was speaking, the monotonous hum of his life being planned all around him. The two said nothing and showed no emotion, wearing the same searching faces and thoughtful brows as they transcribed the whole scene on the paper covered clipboards in their laps. Walter wondered how they could be writing so much. He was being agreeably predictable like he knew they wanted.

"Uh, yeah, certainly," he heard himself say. The new nurses jotted down a few sentences. The head nurse smiled. Walter responded with an empty stare. The room was quiet, waiting. The head nurse shifted some, grinning awkwardly.

"Well...?" she cued Walter.

"Oh, right." Walter cleared his throat. "I, uh — let's see here..." Walter thought of what to say. He hadn't been paying attention. He was lost and close to being called out for it, a kid in the classroom searching in the back corner of his mind to recall something, *anything.* He squinted his eyes and stared into the living room nothingness to make it appear as if he was pondering the nurse's words. Loose connections, short-term recollections, and memories of therapies past were neurons firing to nowhere. Searching, searching, he tried to remember how it was all supposed to go.

Talk, interact, connect — they hold the key to your happiness.

There was a formula to it.

Normalcy, forgetfulness, lingering self-doubt: all complete with a nice set of goals.

"Lately I've really been working on my emotional self-control," Walter declared, "and it's very hard for me." The nurses were surprised at Walter's level of engagement.

"Go on," the head nurse implored.

"Well," Walter heard himself saying, "there's just so much pain, and too many memories...." Walter talked for some time, not really listening to himself. All he knew was that his nurses were satisfied. As he went through his list of talking points, gestures, and buzz phrases, he stole glances at the new guys. He could neither remember nor forget them, and it drove him insane. "....ya see," said Walter, imitating a genuinely concerned and self-aware patient, "I externalize my fears and that causes me to lash out at my teammates, even my daughter."

Who the fuck are these two?

"....and so I get angry with the ones closest to me, and I envision that they're out to get me, and I retreat into deeper fear, and the whole cycle starts all over again."
I know these bastards.

"What's one measurable goal we can make?

I know 'em, I swear to God I do.

"Well, I was thinking about tracking how well I stick to my regimen. Maybe I can make a daily log or something."

I know these sonsabitches.

"Walter! That would be an excellent goal, my friend!"

But from where?

Walter smiled and nodded his head to acknowledge the praise, feeling an internal sigh of relief at having navigated out of the controlled interaction. He looked fully upon the faces of the two new nurses for the first time. They didn't look as familiar to him.

Maybe I'm losin' it...

The one on the left reached up from his pad of paper to itch his ear.

Wait a second.

Walter watched the man dig into his ear, mumbling something.

One goddamn second.

To Walter, it looked like a dark haired man adjusting an earpiece.

Holy shit.

He flinched. They noticed, meeting him with an icy stare. They raised their pencils, ready to write, looking dissatisfied.

It's them.

They watched him with stone-faces. Walter worked on his emotional self-control. It was hard.

He gulped.

The two black haired nurses broke their stare and scribbled tenaciously on their clipboards. They glanced upward at Walter only to frown and write more. Walter tried to ignore them, continuing his conversation with the head nurse.

"I feel I could use some strategies."

No black suit, no blacker Impala; didn't recognize 'em...

"We can begin planning some of those now, and you can develop them with the rest of your team later on at your group meeting."

Walter retreated into his head, consumed. He didn't know what he or anyone else was saying, only that they were taking turns talking.

"....and I almost forgot!" cried the head nurse. "Walter, please accept my apology. These two will be joining our team. They unfortunately couldn't make our morning meeting but will be instrumental in certain parts of your daily regimen from here on out."

Walter got up to shake the hands of the two new nurses over the drone of introductory courtesies, quick pleasantries, and forced smiles. He sat back down.

"We're very excited to join the team," one of them remarked before clearing his throat, "and I'm looking forward to helping monitor your progress."

Walter smiled weakly.

Fuck it. They can be here when it all goes down.
And I gotta surprise for their buddies, too

XX

I'm walking down the dusty trail to the village square, people all around me, just black eyes, bones and rags. They're farmers and they didn't get a good yield this year — they hardly got shit at all. The war saw to that. We saw to the rest: we, the conquerors. My standard issue combat boots leave imprints in the dirt, but I can't see them because I'm looking straight ahead, focusing on my mission, my orders, suppressing all the rest. I walk coolly down the path, and I know I'm in control. Sobbing flutters and dies, then mothers cry again. They're holding their children close, wrapped in their rags, trying to protect them and knowing they can't. In my periphery I can see one mother specifically, her daughter and son wrapped in her raggedy blanket, strong jaw still, wide nostrils flaring, dark eyes piercing my skin. She's not crying. Somehow it's more unsettling. I walk down the road past the crowd. They're all shoeless and caked in dirt. I can feel the heaviness of their sorrow. A toothless grandmother falls to her knees on the side of the road, breaking my concentration. I glance down and see her tragic bony figure begging me for mercy in some language I don't understand. I lift my shoe away from her and snarl, telling myself I'm disgusted and not heartbroken. She's a desperate bitch and I spit in her direction.

I keep walking through the rows of women and their children. The men are in the center, tied at gunpoint and awaiting execution. I look at them and harden my heart, ignoring the cold empty stares of the motherless ragamuffins toward the end of the row. I tell myself the men are to blame: they're scum and they hate the United States, they hate our freedoms and want to punish us for them. They're a threat to you, and me: they hate my little Evee for being cute and free and they want to kill her, the goddamn radical bastards — and I will kill 'em all, send 'em right straight to hell with them American hatin' gods of theirs. Their nasty complicit women will suffer, underhanded manipulative crybabies in rags trying to make me feel bad for their mistakes. And their children —

I look to the center and see the rebel daughter on her bony knees, little arms tied tight behind her back: she can't be more than twelve years old. Her brown hair ruffles in the wind. She stares at me across the killing field with soft eyes that penetrate.

— And their children are just as guilty.

I grit my teeth and walk with more dedication toward her, but I look beyond her and back at the men. They're bandits, they're communists, they're terrorists, they're criminals, they're brown.

Her eyes are calling me a liar, and I can't look away from her. It scares me, and the fear of losing control makes me angry. I reach for my holster, and she doesn't flinch. The crowd gasps in horror as I draw my pistol and point it at the little girl's skull, marching towards her, only a few feet away. I bring the pistol to her forehead, and I can see all of the details of the gun and my fingers wrapped around the trigger, the tendon of my forefinger running back along my flexing forearm, my arm hair running along and under the sleeves of the fatigues. I feel their pleading eyes on my back and I press the barrel hard into her forehead. Her head tilts back slightly and her skin gives a little until I can feel the bone. I can see every little line and detail of her face — the rich color of her beautiful eyes and how her brown hair falls softly over them. Death is staring at her, and she's calm. I grit my teeth because I know she's stronger than me. I'm about to pull the trigger when I hear a desperate voice cry out from the crowd. It makes me jump a little. It's her father. I start to think about how this makes me feel.

And then I blow her fucking brains out.

The blood and bits of skull and tissue splatter all over me. I know what the inside of her head looks like.

I drop my gun and look at my hands and there's blood all over them. I feel a suffocating heaviness. Somebody — one of the troops — comes up to me, placing his hand on my shoulder to reassure me.

"She had brown hair, and blue-gray eyes, just like little Evee..." I lament to the ground.

"Come on buddy," says a voice I recognize, "we got more killing to do."

I look up, my doleful eyes meeting Robert's face.

"They'll take care of us later..."

Walter lay still in his sweat-soaked bed, wide eyes of regret fixed on the ceiling. He had everything he needed except the Drain-o.

XXI

On any given Tuesday, Walter had two small windows of free time. One was before bed. He'd use that time to finalize everything. The other came earlier, during the eight minute period (allowing two minutes for transitions) between wrapping up his morning activity session — which ended at 11:50 — and his lunch, which was always at noon. Walter wanted to use this time to arrange and store the contents of his old icepacks. He had a lot to do, but if he was quick enough, eight minutes would be more than sufficient. That is, if his session ended on time.

It was strange. Walter knew it wouldn't all be over by 11:50. He felt a little paranoid, but he suspected the nurses knew it, too.

"Walter, I'm intrigued by the line…what was it? 'Happiness is a choice/Commit to blissful ignorance'. What were you going for there?" The nurses smiled in anticipation. Walter clutched his poem — the culmination of his Tuesday morning activity session. He brought it to his nose, "Uh, let's see here…" he grumbled.

11:47 and she's still analyzing the third stanza of my poem. Jesus Christ.

"I reckon I meant...."

I sugarcoat the line. I tell them what they wanna hear. Just shut the fuck up and let me get ready.

"Wow Walter! How profound!" exclaimed one of the nurses, "how did you come up with that?"

Walter grew anxious. He sensed their not-so-subtle attempts to psychoanalyze him. If his plan was going to work, he only had 1 minute and 46 seconds to explain it all away.

"I guess because a lot of people are happy and ignorant," responded Walter matter-of-factly. The two new male nurses transcribed his answer with interest. His heart sank when he saw them. Even when he was as literal as possible, his team knew how to read into things.

"Hmm..." wondered the head nurse, patronizing softly. "Would you say you are happy, Walter?"

Walter could feel the tick of each second cutting into him, nudging him closer and closer to 11:50. 11:50 was a clear limitation on what would pass, the beginning of a new end, and he wanted it to square up evenly. He didn't know what would happen if he got pushed past the limit. He figured he'd dissolve.

"Yes."

The nurses exchanged glances of surprise, a thin veneer for their doubt.

"Really?" asked one of the new male nurses.

"Yes." Walter looked into his eyes. "And I'll tell you why. For the first time in a long time I am invested in my well-being, and I'm taking steps to ensure it."

The rest of the room waited for him to continue.

"I'm setting goals as well as time frames for these goals, and it involves a lot of plo—I mean planning," Walter corrected. The nurses looked at him curiously. Walter sensed suspicion. He wondered how much they knew.

"Such as?" one of the dark haired male nurses asked expectantly, pen raised. It was 11:49. Walter could feel the hot air rise up inside of him. He needed to say something clever, concise, and conclusive, and he needed to do it in less than one minute. He sifted through the fog of his memory bank and recalled a goal he set the morning before.

"I've really been trying to stick to my regimen, minute by minute. I even keep a daily log now," he said with believable conviction.

It was all too perfect.

"Not only does it help me maintain," Walter went on, "but it maximizes my day, which makes me happy." The nurses nodded with approval. The hot air in Walter's chest gave way to an air of contentment. He did it.

"Speaking of which," smiled the head nurse, "It just hit 11:50. If we want you to be successful, we better let you go."

You have no idea.

24 seconds later, Walter uttered his last courtesy and headed straight for the bedroom closet. He didn't emerge from his room until 8 seconds before noon. By that time, he had just about everything ready.

....

She was surprised when Walter asked her out to lunch. He claimed that he needed to go to the grocery store and that lunch was secondary, but even that was strange. Typically, she would present a list to Walter, he would grunt, and she'd do the shopping. She shrugged, hoping that it was a sign of Walter's increasing investment.

He waited for her answer in the dim kitchen entryway, the afternoon sunlight eking through the window, metal coffee thermos in his hand. She looked up from the table, smiling.

"We could be back by two," he sputtered, "and I still could get a thirty minute nap in before preparing for group therapy at three."

She studied him, his raised pleading brow.

"Of course," she said warmly. "Wherever you want to go, Dad." Walter's body flexed into a quick excited "yes!", his fist pumped and clenched. She laughed softly through her nose. He turned and disappeared into the living room, returning in his faded gray jacket and American flag cap, her coat wrapped in one arm. Hand still clutching the coffee thermos, he held out the other ceremoniously.

"Ready pumkin?"

She cheerfully pushed herself out from the table, rising with grace from her seat, bending over and dusting off her blue jeans. She looked up at Walter with glowing cheeks and beauty in her eyes.

Don't look into them.

"Ready Dad!" she smiled, reaching for her coat. He half dropped it — letting go before her grip was sure — darting nervously towards the garage. The door opened and she could hear the resonant clatter of Walter descending the steps and stumbling over loose ends and cuss words. She slid towards the door, trying not to laugh as the garage melee echoed into the kitchen. She plunged her hand into the darkness and flicked the light switch. The dim light cast afternoon shadows around the makeshift shelves and hanging trinkets — swords, a moose head, WWII replica rifle, badminton racket, some tools, and his army apparel hung overhead piles of junk, memorabilia, trophies and trash, some of it useable but having spent years unused, some of it totally useless.

She looked down from where she stood to see a wrestling Walter tangled in broken fishing poles and old flat-tire Schwinns, half-empty oil cans at his feet. She came to him; it made him uneasy, and he struggled deeper into the knots of spokes and line:

"Goddamninfrmnshitmongrnsonnofabitch..."

She tried untangling him, but he lost his patience. He waved his limbs frantically and thrashed about the mess, crashing into toolboxes and trashcans, flexing and straining and trying to act cool but growing red and taught. He ripped and gasped, cutting through the line and shedding the knots with one last "JESUS CHRIST!", a rusty bike falling at his feet. He was panting but feigned nonchalance as he brushed himself off and stepped out of the final weave of fishing wire and junk, still holding coffee thermos tight as he headed for the driver's side door.

Every single time, she sighed, shaking her head.

"Dad," she began.

He hadn't driven his car in years. She wouldn't let him. He was old, delirious, and medicated: in short, a hazard. Still, she pitied him, his age and dying freedoms.

Walter stopped near the door, close enough to see his distorted reflection in the darkened light of the window. He felt the beginnings of shame, slow and smoldering. He grumbled something about sacrifice for his country and old era entitlement.

The car keys jingled as she moved towards the driver side door. He checked his pockets for show before casting a longing gaze upon the shadowed Cadillac. It was American made, and he was proud. If only he could drive it.

"Come on," she snapped. Defeated, he shuffled around the car. A good daughter usually trails behind her aging father to help him into his seat, but the success of her power trip told her to shake her head and grunt in disgust, all the while smiling inside. He reached the door, sighing with ennui as he tugged at the handle — it slipped from his apathetic fingers. He made them just firm enough to grab the silver latch, opening the door to where he stood. He set his coffee thermos on the garage floor, lining up laterally with the car so he could ease in, first one side of his body, then the other. She pursed her lips and exhaled through her nose, exasperated with Walter and his sad, torpid movements. She felt a little guilty for not helping him but settled for a loud sigh, directing any excess shame toward him. He was just now ducking his head under the roof, his left leg up to the hip inside the car. He hung precariously before committing to sitting down, careful moments spent calculating when his rear could rest, anticipation growing, back and brittle joints cracking as his slow body inched toward the seat. Finally, his ass over the seat and only centimeters away, he sort of plopped down with the attitude of "Well, fuck it," sighing, grunting, and giving up in one big, geriatric motion. Grumbling some more, he tried to move his right leg inside the car. It was incredibly stiff; he extended his arms out to half pick it up. He finagled it inside and let it drop down by the floor mat. He reached down and grabbed his coffee thermos, placing it on the floor at his feet, all settled in but the door hanging open. He sat for a second, catching his breath before tipping over in his seat and leaning the upper half of his body out the door, reaching for the internal handle with both arms, his bent and gnarled fingers stretching for grip. He caught it with two knotty fingers and pulled it toward him. After a few tries, the low whine of the creaking metal spring gave way to angry mumbles and the soft slam of the Cadillac door. Walter straightened up and looked at himself in the mirror. He looked old, tired, helpless.

"Where you taking me, Dad?"

To hell.

"What was that?" she smiled.

"I said, 'Well...'"

They pulled up right next to Walter's favorite diner, parking in the handicap spot. She got out of the car, walking around to help him this time. Walter cracked open the door and told her he didn't need any help, giving a weak kick to open it the rest of the way. The heavy door recoiled from the spring and swung back towards his leg hanging on the frame; luckily, she grabbed the handle just in time and pulled it safely open past the hinges. Walter grumbled and shifted angrily like she wasn't helping. He turned and swung both legs out of the car, his Velcro shoes hanging above the pavement as his jeans rode up to expose his paper white ankles. He let his shoes touch the ground slowly. One frail hand reached for the assist handle (commonly referred to as the "oh shit bar"), the other turned palm-down on the cushion for support. He pulled on the bar with feeble determination as his body rose and his bony palm on the seat gradually extended to the fingertips. He pulled harder, feeling reckless for putting all of his weight on the assist handle, hanging perilously for one second before he gave one last heave, simultaneously raising his shoulders and falling back on the solid support of the door frame.

She rushed over to help him. Out of breath, he half-heartedly shooed her away; at the same time, he leaned into her embrace. They shuffled away from the door. She closed it with one hand, holding Walter up in the other. His tragic figure hunched over, shoes scraping the ground, she led him into the diner. It was emasculating and he hated it.

He lightened up a little standing in the warmth of the entryway, the sound of the glass door closing behind him as he looked up to meet the brusque half-frown of the cold, fifty-something cook-owner-waitress.

"Heya Brenda, whaddya say?" Walter grinned amiably.

"Sit where you like," she muttered in an indifferent attempt to be friendly. Walter laughed and shuffled past, shaking his head as he slid into the faded red vinyl booth, his date sitting down across from him. He reached for the menu — over the plain white tabletop and towards the stack of sugar packets, condiments, and metal-ringed pie descriptions — though he had no intentions of looking at it. Instead, he slid it under his knuckles, drumming on its cheap laminate with the ready smile of a patron prepared to order, his eyes wandering across the diner. The paneled walls were covered with proverbial diner knickknacks: tin signs reading "World Famous Potato Salad," "Enjoy Coke, 5¢," and "Drink Ted's Famous Creamy Root Beer,"; memorabilia from random celebrities who *might* have eaten there; a few old washboards and framed newspaper clippings, some more relevant than others. Walter looked towards the white countertop bar that stretched around the kitchen. A small sizzle wafted from the back, dying slowly over the faded red stool tops. He smiled.

Walter returned his gaze to the beautiful woman sitting across from him. She squinted hard at the menu, puzzled and muttering to herself in hushed tones. She didn't know what to get.

Jesus...

Walter shook his head in mild disgust and went back to drinking in his beloved American diner. He looked across the room at the other customers from his easy lean in the booth, one of the younger, grittier female waitresses passing through his view. He chuckled half-mindedly at her punky attitude as she left the scene in his eye to reveal four big-hoss-type good ol' boy Hoosiers hunched over a table, all football, camo, gravy and pork. They looked like giants and talked with mouthfuls about hunting and politics, sideburns and beards down their fat, strong faces. Walter contemplated them momentarily before directing his gaze to another table, this one with two old married couples. They were the type to come Sundays after church and Tuesdays after doctor's appointments, gray and probably in their late 80s, drinking plenty of coffee. He looked back to the countertop, this time noticing a young man seated there; he gazed beyond him and into the slow rush of the kitchen.

"What wouldya like?" Walter turned to see Brenda next to the table, gruff with arms folded.

"I'd like for you to smile every now and again." Walter cackled. Brenda tried hard not to smile, and her face didn't change much.

"No, I mean what'll it be?" she retorted.

"*It'll be* nice if you lighten up darlin', hehehe." Brenda couldn't help but chortle and shake her head.

"There we go, there's that smile!" exclaimed Walter. His companion started to admonish him from across the booth, but Brenda cut her off.

"You better settle down old man, or I'll have to rough you up a bit," Brenda grinned.

"Oh-ho! I'd like that too much! Hehehehehe." Brenda raised her eyebrows at Walter.

"Well then, I might have to get Sam to throw you out, and she's just downright mean."

Walter looked across the beige carpet of the restaurant at the punky waitress. She heard her name and glared back at him. He faked a big, fearful gulp before turning back to Brenda, laughing hard at her wry grin.

"Well, you know what I'm eating," he said through a chuckle, "but this one over here..." He thumbed towards his date pouring over the simple menu with scrunched brow, mumbling ingredients to diner foods.

"I'll just have a bagel and some coffee," she concluded, handing her menu to Brenda as Walter rolled his eyes.

"Coffee for the both of you, then?" Brenda asked,

glancing towards Walter as she grabbed his menu.

"A'cour—"

"None for him, thank you."

Walter looked across the table with confusion and contempt. "What?" she defended. "You have that whole thermos in the car."

"Ahh," he said, turning toward Brenda with a shrug, "she's right."

Damn.

"I'll just stick to water and great service then," he winked.

Gotta play like it ain't empty...

"Coffee and bagel for the lady and the usual punch in the nose for the old man, got it," Brenda joked dryly as she walked away.

"That Brenda," Walter laughed, shaking his head before turning his attention back inside the booth. "So kiddo, whatdya know?" She smiled and started talking. Walter nodded his head customarily, grinning and looking interested like any aging father would — saying things like "wow" and "how about that?" He found it hard to concentrate in the ambience of the diner, one of the few places he loved.

From one table: "I don't wanna live in *his* America."

From another: "I sure hope Betty gets it together."

The restaurant buzzed with soft murmurs of fear and good intentions:

"Hopefully I'll get paid enough this month ta...."

"She'll come around, she has her family and the Lord...."

Anxiety, complacency: the order of the hushed diner conversations of Middle America, places where people smile, eat, wave, and worry. Walter nodded as she finished talking, a goofy look on his face as he pretended to engage.

"....annnyway, our food should be here by now, right Dad?" she asked after a brief pause.

"Hold on there," chided Walter, "give those ladies some time back there, they work sa'damn hard."

She grinned. She always did appreciate Walter's good humor.

"It's all us womenfolk know how to do," she replied, laughing tone but genuine intent.

"Boy I guess!" cackled Walter, "you and that team a nurses damn near run me to death!" She couldn't tell if he was sarcastic or bitter, and neither could he. He smirked mysteriously and gazed into the distance.

The sound of porcelain plates set down and sliding across restaurant tables snapped his reverie.

"Thank ya Brenda," he smiled.

"Anything else?" Brenda said flatly. They shook their heads politely, but she was already gone. Walter looked down at his Tuesday brunch, clapping his hands and rubbing them together, the sizzle of real sausage filling his nostrils as he drooled over a hefty plate of biscuits and gravy.

....

The Cadillac made its careful circle through the crowded straights of the mega-mart parking lot, Walter clutching the empty coffee thermos and every so often taking phantom sips. The lot was full of American shoppers clogging traffic, crossing yellow striped lanes to either emerge or disappear from giant automatic glass doors. She putted along, aware of cars and pedestrians distracted by bargains, looking for the perfect spot. Every space near the front was taken by some sort of truck, suburban, minivan, or rusting Oldsmobile. There were a few empty spaces in the back, but she knew Walter would complain and for the most part be justified in doing so.

"Are these people pulling out, er, what's the deal here?" she muttered. She eased to an idle, seeing movement inside the windows of a maroon minivan and waiting for the conclusion. The door slid open from the inside and a gaggle of blue collar kids in flannels and pajamas came hopping out, their fat, ranch-eating parents left behind to struggle between tight spaces and parked cars.

"Damn!" She shook her head and hit the gas, immediately breaking hard for two old, gray-haired shuffling shoe-gazers. She grew tense. She could never just get in and out. By the time the old couple had left her path, scores of other shoppers walked wantonly in front and around her vehicle, and she knew she was drowning in the mundane details of consumerist America.

She edged the car forward, crossing the crowded, yellow-striped pedestrian lanes once more before circling around into a new row. She looked from side to side shrewdly.

"Aha!"

There, only three spots from where she idled and a mere twenty-four feet away from the occupied handicapped section near the front entrance, sat an empty space. She shook with giddiness and squealed, small and short. Walter felt the inertia of the accelerating car push his weight back into the seat, her smile growing bigger as they neared the space. She slowed down, the anticipation of pulling into the perfect spot warming her blood as she prepared to turn the wheel.

SKERRRR!

"Fucker!" she spat as a slightly used Taurus swerved in front of her to steal the spot, screeching its tires and narrowly avoiding a collision for the sake of a shopper's convenience. She floored the gas pedal — pushing Walter back into the seat — driving recklessly to find the next available parking space.

That'll show 'em.

She didn't care that it was all the way in the back. She swung in fast, pissed off and feeling better about herself, though she could still feel her body clench as she anticipated the old man's complaints. She turned and glared at him with a look like "Say something!", but Walter had already fumbled for the door, opened it, closed it, realized he forgot his empty thermos — the center of his whole outing — and re-entered the car to nervously snatch it back before shutting the door behind him, leaving her to challenge the empty seat. She chortled, partly at her own ego trip but mostly at Walter's erratic behavior. She got out of the car, chasing after him as his bent and receding frame shuffled down the lane and toward the superstore. She quickly caught up to him and his scuttling little legs — he moved faster as if to get away. She kept pace with ease.

They passed parked cars and random carts, empty grates and dawdling Midwestern consumers, the occasional truck or Suburban exhaling impatiently from behind the unwitting shoppers. The October sun shone weakly on the blue mega-mart font, blocked letters reading "GROCERY" hanging on the colorless brick above the nearest awning. The pair headed towards the entrance like moths to lights, passing tiny hordes of people walking in and out, talking on cell phones, staring at shoes, looking ahead with empty eyes or otherwise dazed and mindless. Eventually they reached the yellow pedestrian stripes.

"Dad!"

She reached for Walter's sleeve but he pulled away, trudging across the soft anarchy of the striped lane in front of an angry car grill, shouting driver stopping just in time. She gasped, scampering across the lane and throwing an embarrassed side wave toward the stopped car as she mouthed "I'm sorry." Walter continued unfazed towards the shadowed alcove of outdoor seasonal deals. Harvest and Halloween décor, pumpkins and scarecrows, cornucopias, and other late fall goods made lines and piles in and out of boxes near the pale light of the giant automatic glass doors. The doors slid open and swallowed him.

The fluorescent light blinded Walter. For a few seconds he stood dazed at the entrance, his eyes trying to adjust to the pale lit, white-walled, shiny mart-mopped glow of consumerist Shangri-La. He took a few steps forward, unaware that the old, smiling greeter had been addressing him since he came in, the murmur of her voice dying as he shuffled beyond her stickered vest and the cart corral, past the proverbial superstore café and towards the seemingly infinite rows of products and sales. He stopped near the queue for the register, scratching his head, puzzled. He squinted at the first aisle and then beyond.

The glass doors opened behind Walter; his companion walked briskly through them, spotting him in his trance.

All this shit here and probably none of it American made and I hate it and I don't know where a goddamn thing is: candy and clothes and jewelry and birthday cards, all jumbled together, to my right I think is where they group all of the groceries...let's see here...gadgets that way, liquor over there...what does that say...?? Ok, hygiene products over thattaway...let's see...

She reached for his shoulder as she approached him with the cart.

Fuck it ta hell, the cleaner's in the back.

"Dad!"
Shit!
Walter jumped, startled, clutching the empty coffee thermos with white knuckles.

She knows, my goddamn alibi and my motive don't align and she fucking kno—

"Are you listening to me? Hey, are you ok?" She was in front of him now, looking into his lost eyes, worried.

"Huh?" Walter shook his head.

"I said, 'the groceries are over this way, let's get the produce first,'" she repeated with concern.

"Oh," muttered Walter lamely, "sure."

She sighed and pushed the cart away from him. He gave one last look towards the cleaning products — distant and secluded, aisles of shelves and obstacles from where he stood — before turning to catch up with her.

FFFFFFWWOO

He stopped short and sucked in his little belly as a suburban cartfull of groceries whisked past, pushed hard and indifferent by a house-mom on a cell phone appeasing her screaming daughter perched atop the cart basket. He shook his head and continued toward his companion sizing up zucchinis in the produce section. Shuffling across the tile, his eyes were bathed in the beauty of the coordinated color schemes of GMO painted plants. He stopped for a second, watching with interest as the other shoppers wandered up to boxed shelves of fruits and veggies, sweaty fingers passing over the same green, red, and purple skins plucked by migrant workers and modern day slaves. He turned to see a twenty-something couple, man with hipster glasses, tight corduroys and sweater holding hands with woman in flannel and skinny jeans, using their free fingers to search through tri-colored peppers.

Probably taste like servitude and bone marrow...

Walter switched his gaze to a sweet, old woman — the type to carry a pocketbook full of coins — bent over in a big fall sweater and fumbling through tomatoes.

Searching through tendons and sweat, old maid has no idea....

He looked around, trapped in a nightmarish megastore carnival: shoppers browsing through plants and human tissue, American capitalism and conglomerate farm politics, thirty-something singles going "organic," old ladies smiling and paying for death — he tried to shake it all from his mind. Eyes between sideways looks and a dream, he ran into her at the produce bin, causing her to drop her prized zucchini in the shuffle. She tried to conceal her rage, but Walter detected her discontent.

"I really don't eat that shit anyway," he offered.

"I do," she responded, cold and motionless.

"Oh."

"Forget it," she sighed, starting to push the cart through the aisle with Walter at her heel, "let's get your things." He shrugged as he followed her past coolers of carrots and mushrooms and spinach, the tile of the produce section giving way to the dim, warm ambience of the bakery. Stacks of factory bread — preservative white, split wheat, whole grain, nutbread, sourdough, small, big, thin and thick — sat neatly in predetermined rows. Walter watched as she bent over the racks, searching with hand near mouth and furrowed brow.

Fuck those little kiddie-sized chemical loaves of white...

Her hand passed over the white bread, hovering near the gritty wheat with all the nuts inside.

Jesus, I just threw up in my mouth.

Walter turned to look out across the rowed mélange of processed barley and gluten — over the loaves, buns, and bagels, the pita and artisan breads, the cookie assortments — noticing the glass displays of the mega-mart Baker's Corner. Underpaid workers watched over cakes, pies, scones, doughnuts, and other superstore delicacies. Some stood proud by the display cases with upselling smiles and droopy baker's hats, but even they were secretly miserable.

"Just get the regular wheat bread," Walter said, empty.

....

Steady now old man. You don't want to ruin it now do you? No, it's been a long time comin', and you won't let a little factory farmed meat make you jump and rush the plan...

Passing through the butcher section, he began to lose his mind.

Been eatin' tofu so long I forgot what steak looks like. Jesus Christ I'm going soft.

He could see the minimum wage white butcher coats stained in blood, floating behind a counter of chicken, beef, and pork; he could feel the chill from the coolers and freezers and felt like the tightly packaged meat all around him.

Get a grip old man. It's the same old meat. The same old butchered-ass, hormone injected, feces ridden, cage-crammed, ozone killing, water wasting, corralled and cut by poor immigrant and white working man salmonella sardine-packed USDA meat.

He turned anxiously toward her, staring at the side of her face as they walked. She looked complacent, just like everyone else.

And I ain't no different from it, here in these aisles crammed
next to pork and beef and my 00 Agent Daughter, freezing cold
and watching alla these goddamn idiots buying shit that will
kill them in the end — and I ain't no better, cause I'm here. I
ain't no better. I'm doing the same thing, in the same place, at
the same time, all of us fucking cowards in a big mindless fuck-
off superstore shopping spree, buying products made by kids or
poor people driving wages down, using social security, EBT,
and depressed wage money in a big cyclical shitfuck economy
and walking around talking about the good old days. I'm just
like them, a spineless lover of convenience, yes, and that's all
we are, and that's all we'll ever be —

Eggs by chickens stuffed 5 to a cage...
> *—Stained sweater unwashed hair and dirty pajama*
> *pants walking aimlessly through the dairy.*
Cheese from bloodmilk...
> *—Successful entrepreneur with suit and tie and black*
> *shoe gloss, cart overflowing with steaks and liquor.*

It will win.
 It will win.
  I will fail...

Walter breathed deeply and tried to find reality. He knew
that heavy doses of consumerism were not good for the

psyche. It was the heart of this place, the megastore, beating and turning him mad. He doubted his plan — all of it. His sweaty palms grew sore from their hard, anxious grip on the thermos.

"Dad, did you drink all of that coffee?" her voice echoed in Walter's brain.

What coffee?

"Is that why you've been acting so strange, Dad?"

Strange? She knows. Jesus H I'm acting different and she's on to me, she's hip to the whole scene and they got me straight cheesed on the raw deal—

She put one hand on Walter's shoulder and reached out for the thermos with the other.

Oh God oh God oh God oh God—

"Wow! That's a lot of coffee for you to drink at once," she remarked, feeling the emptiness of the thermos. "Maybe you should find the bathroom."

Wait, what?

"....wash up, maybe drink some water from the fountain."

My...alibi?

"....you know, that sort of thing."

"You're right Evee," mumbled Walter, darting away. "I'm dehydrated as hell and gotta piss real bad."

I can't believe this!

Walter moved past wandering Tuesday Hoosiers pushing carts, carrying baskets, consuming. He headed towards the back of the building, the last remnants of the groceries fading into neat sections of home-products and clothes. He turned the corner of the tiled walkway. Women in their forties shopped for new socks for their husbands and warm clothes for kids soon preparing for winter: if she makes enough back in savings, she might be able to buy that hip new scarf to show the girls at work. A gruff, middle-aged working man — body too old for the grit of manual labor best left to young men — standing in raggedy jeans and holey soles in front of rows of work boots: he thinks if he can find the right pair he can wait out his pension. Walter surveyed the carpeted clothing areas from the tile, not sure what to make of his fellow mega-store Americans. A few steps more took him past furniture and other household miscellanea, every so often a young man plopping down in a test chair to humor his girlfriend or a gaggle of kids running through rows and jumping on cushions, comparison shoppers sifting through picture frames and homey ornaments.

"OOOFF!"

Distracted and looking sideways, Walter crashed into the $5 bin of overflowing mega-deal movies in front of him. The haphazard pile jumbled and spilled, movie cases hitting the tile with high-smacking echoes. Walter gripped the metallic sides of the bin to keep from falling down. An employee ran over to assist him, reaching for his shoulder.

"Fuck off!" snapped Walter as he flung his arm in defense.

"Sir, I'm here to help," he offered, backing away from Walter and nervously gathering movie cases in both arms.

"I'm beyond help," he said darkly.

The employee looked at him fearfully, his hand gravitating towards his store radio. Walter left, passing bratty kids demanding the latest video games from their parents, making one-sided bargains and deals for rewards woefully disproportionate to their mediocre achievements.

Fuck electronics.

Fortunately for Walter, the toy section was obstructed. He continued toward the corner of the store, searching for the cleaning supplies; instead he found sporting goods, rifles, car products, and fat shoppers in college sweaters boosting their favorite teams from Indiana, Michigan, or Ohio. He doubled back in a new row, unwittingly stumbling into the last aisle in the rear of the store. Chia-pets, tanks full of exotic fish or frogs, TVs, and other anomalies lined the walls.

Where am I?

He spun slowly, eyes full of fluorescence and assorted imports. He was lost.

Been gone so long now I actually do gotta piss.

The restroom in any superstore always used to be in the back; some newer stores, however, place them in the front. Regardless, Walter had no idea where he was, and he had to piss, real bad. He circled through the store, bent low to hold it in rather than to ease his chronic back pain.

Alcohol, no,
birthday cards, no,
jewelry, no,
winter wear, no,
baseball gloves, no
—wait, have I been here before...?
Hmmm....
Savings on fall wear, no,

168

candy, no,

landscaping, no,

pills, FUCK NO,

paper towel, no,

JESUS CHRIST, WHERE IS THE FUCKING BATHROOM?!

Walter couldn't take it. There was no way. He was ready to pee his pants.

Then, he saw it.

His frantic, circuitous search for the restroom had sent him stumbling unawares towards the cleaning supplies. Walter now stood eye-level with the Drain-o.

He clutched the thermos, forgetting all about his urinary quest. His eyes bore through the thick font on the Drain-o label and the red paint of the bottle; he could see the chemical colored liquid sloshing around inside. It was powerful, dangerous, volatile. It was just what he needed.

Walter looked over his left shoulder, then slowly over his right. He was alone. Lifting his left hand and placing it on the thermos lid, he carefully twisted the top. Overcautious, quiet: just unscrewing the lid took a few minutes. When he was finished, he checked his surroundings again — found he was still alone — and meticulously placed thermos and lid on an open space one shelf down from his coveted Drain-o. His heart beat fast as his outstretched fingers gravitated toward the bottle.

   ...

    ...

    ...He retracted his hands.

Can't, I just can't.

Walter hadn't actually dealt with this part of the plan. He didn't think he'd make it this far.

I ain't no thief, swear to God I ain't...but what else can I do?

He had to steal it. It was either that or walk up absentmindedly with a bottle full of capricious chemicals and toss it in the cart.

You know, no biggie.

He knew that wouldn't work.

Just plain asinine.

So, there it was. If a consumer wants a product in any American superstore, they have two possible courses of action: the first, to exchange it for legal tender; the second, to steal it. After twenty-four years of silent plotting, wiping down the mega-mart was his only option. Walter reached for the Drain-o, pulling it gingerly off the shelf.

I been alotta things, but I ain't never been no thief...

He turned the bottle over in his hands.

I just can't do it...

He searched the label.

"Manufactured in Louisiana".

Walter stood in the middle of the aisle, reading product information and having an existential crisis:

A man just doesn't steal.
—Made in Louisiana, say, rivers run through there...

The sides of his vision turned to sand, and he was nothing but his sticky fingers and moral dilemma spelled out in small company font.

T'ain't right!
—And the old folk, rural folk and the old descendants of slaves

own proud pieces of shit land on those rivers...

She was tired of waiting on Walter near the registers.
He had been gone a long time.

I beena bad father, a killer, and a lunatic, but I never stole.

She left to find him.

*—But the rivers are polluted; they taste like disease, like the
soil, like everything in Cancer Alley...*

He gripped the bottle harder.

I swear to God I never stole a penny, a fucking crumb, nothing!

She wandered toward the back corner of the building.

*—But rivers don't run polluted. Corporations pay people
minimum wage to handle toxic chemicals and dump the left
overs. And the finished product is the red container you're
holding, bottled and sold at $6.99 a pop: lotta profit when you
gotta fucking Texas Tea style goldmine of drain-clearing elixir
in your basement, poor people working for ya and free
riverside disposal. And the people won't complain, because
they might not know: hell, even if they did, America needs its*

sinks and toilets and drains cleaned goddamnit!

He suddenly didn't feel so bad about stealing from the mega-mart.

—Just like America needs its subsidized groceries, its clothes from Vietnam and Guatemala and Bangladesh, its cheap toys and Chinese cookware. Just like it needs its liquor and pills and jewelry and magazines and mega-mart mind warps...

He found himself unscrewing the lid of the Drain-o.

Am I really doing this?

She was five aisles away, walking slowly and looking down each straight for signs of Walter.

—Selling everything back lowball because they pay their pawns enough to qualify for food stamps, making millions on millions off misery, ruling the fucking world with swinging dicks and discounts...

He grabbed his coffee thermos off the shelf.

Hell yeah I'm doing this.

Walter poured the contents of the bottle into the thermos.

I'm damn near obligated to do this.

She was four aisles away.

My goddamn revolutionary duty as an American!

....two aisles away.

FUCK THE MEGA-MART.

....looking down the adjacent aisle—

Walter carefully caught the last drip to fill the thermos, positing the half-closed Drain-o bottle back onto the shelf. She rounded the corner as he finished securing the coffee lid.

"There you are!" she cried. Walter jumped, almost dropping his prize. He looked at her sheepishly as she rushed to where he stood.

"Where have you been?"

Walter stammered. "Well, I, uh — ya see, I, I...uh."

"Forget it," she said through a wry smile, "I'm just glad I found you." She looked up at the shelf, frowning. Walter froze.

She shook her head at the crooked lid of the Drain-o bottle, mumbling mega-mart displeasures. "You ready?" she finally said, turning toward Walter with an incredulous grin.

Walter nodded his head vigorously, feeling antsy. He never did find the bathroom, and he had to piss real bad.

XXII

I know they killed her. She's been dead since it happened, the massacre. She's been dead since then and she's never coming back.

In a way, I helped kill her. Now, her pretty specter haunts my dreams at night.

I know she's dead.
I know she's dead.

So why do I see her with golden sunlit halo on October morning walks? Why do those gentle fingers prepare three meals a day for my ungrateful mouth? Why is she in front of me, chewing thoughtfully at the dinner table with a bright smile in her eyes?

Could it be her?

He looked across the table and tried to remember, tried to make sense of it all.

Could this woman really be...my daughter?

The war ended long before Walter could go home. When he finally made it back stateside, he was relegated to a government building for debriefing — white coats and walls, bright lights and confusion his only recollections. He had no idea how long he was there. He couldn't remember much about the end of the war.

The fog started around the time of his troops' last mission — white, thick, translucent, a dream on the tip of nervous morning tongues — and it didn't fade until he came home. Seeing her was his first and truest memory, the beginning of his postwar waking life: Wednesday, October 24th.

I was there in my corner chair, but I might as well've been sitting on the edge of the earth, it was all so damn hazy. Paralysis in the dim dust, like I'm sleeping but I ain't, in and out of visions and soft snores, the only thing I know for sure is how the chair forms around my body and how my arms and legs sit still. But hell, I've been in and out so goddamn long the chair could either be part of the dream, or part of reality taking new forms in the dream...

Through the heaviness I could sense something, a silhouette through tired eyes, a soft and blurry figure like looking through the shower door. It approached me. I tried and tried to wake up. I squirmed and counted to 3 and clenched, but I was

paralyzed, head to toe. Shadowy fingertips extended slowly,
closer and closer to my face. I felt cold and sick.

"Oh Dad, poor thing."

Another shadow loomed in the background:

"His treatment starts immediately…"

She was only 19 when Walter awoke, wild-eyed and staring at her concerned hand on his shoulder. She furrowed her brow, compassion in her face.

"Who're you with?" he demanded after some time, frowning suspiciously into her beautiful, sad eyes.

They were alone.

She sighed. He studied her face. There was something different about her, something he couldn't quite place. She sensed his befuddlement and tried to ease his pain:

"It's me."

Walter continued to scrutinize her features.

It's all there, but something's missing.

"Your daughter."

One little detail they couldn't possibly copy.

"Your Eve—"

"Your eyes," Walter interjected softly, "they look, different..."

They exchanged quizzical looks in the living room silence.

"So do yours," she answered. "It's been eight years, Dad, and we've both been through so much."

A burning heaviness settled in Walter's lower chest. He hadn't seen his daughter in a long time. He tried to sit taller in his recliner. He wanted to look at her more directly.

"The doctor said you might be a little confused, maybe distrustful at first," she soothed, "but—"

"Doctor?" spouted Walter, "what do you mean, *doctor*? Doctor who?"

"Dr. C will be your lead psychiatrist," she said. "He's a brilliant man, really, very revolutionary ideas and therapies—"

"I've been a part of this man's 'revolution.' Oh yes, I know all about the venerable Dr. Calus..." Walter muttered into his delirious eternity.

"You've never met," she retorted, "and his name is *Dr. C.* You'll get acquainted tomorrow."

Walter gave her a soundless scowl.

"Dad, a lot has happened, and a lot has changed," she began, kneeling down and placing her hands tenderly on Walter's bent knee, "and there's a lot of work to do to get you well again."

Get me well? What does that mean?

"But I'll do whatever it takes, whatever the doctor says, because I want you happy. I just, I—"

Whatever he says?

Walter gazed into her crying eyes. He knew something was wrong.

"Say, pumkin," he started, "what day is today?"

"Wednesday," she sniffled into her blouse.

"No, no — I mean the date," he clarified.

"Oh, I don't know," she mumbled, looking off as if thinking, "the 23rd or 24th... actually it's the 24th — why?"

He searched her confused eyes.

"Oh, I don't know..." Walter measured his words, thinking of whether or not to expose her.

Why? It was your own mother for chrissake!

"No reason," he smiled.

October 24th: anniversary of my wife's death — day my purgatory begins.

"Your treatment starts immediately," she asserted as she rose above him.

She left the room and prepared to call Dr. C. Walter would need intensive therapy and lots of drugs.

XXIII

His whole life was in the twelve minutes between 8:18 and 8:30pm on Tuesday, October 23rd: his second and final window of free time. He had a closet full of powdered aluminum (from the beer cans) and ammonium nitrate (found in old icepacks), and he had to be very careful. He still needed to make two packages with the stolen Drain-o. And, what's more, he had to get it all done before she came knocking on his bedroom door at 8:30:01 sharp. It was a lot of dangerous work to be done in a short amount of time, but it was his only shot at freedom.

Thing about being free is, comes a point where you can't turn back, even if you wanted to.

Walter used up the Drain-o to make two small bombs. He tucked them under his pillow.

Even if you wanted to, they wouldn't take you. You've gone too far.

Walter used the remaining minutes before bed to get dressed, brush his teeth, and get a glass of water. All the while he surreptitiously wandered throughout the house, hiding volatile, time-sensitive containers of aluminum powder and ammonium nitrate in vulnerable cracks, crevices, and shadows. Somehow, he completed his mission undetected, his head lowering onto the soft folds of the pillow in time with her tender knock. He closed his eyes and feigned sleep. The creak of the old oaken door was followed by a stream of curious hallway light. She looked upon him with worry before gently closing the door. Walter smiled in the darkness, his body caught in the slow drag of sleep's gravity.

....

It was our last mission. The war was pretty much over. The enemy was tired, defeated, but they weren't quite ready to give it up. So they sent us in. We went to the birthplace of one of the rebel leaders, his home village. I guess we figured we'd bleed him out, make him feel guilty for his peoples' pain. It was an awful thing to do. But back then, I didn't think. Back then, I just did what I was told.

It was a small farming village, and it wasn't long before we seized their crop, forcing them to surrender. It was easy. Cause of the war, there wasn't much crop to begin with; and secondly, almost all of 'em were women and children. Yep, only a few men who didn't abandon their hometown for romantic dreams and war laurels — we tied 'em up and put 'em on display in the center. We shot one in the back of the head, right away, like BLAM: execution style. I really can't remember why. Honestly, I don't think we even knew who he was. We were there for blood, and we wanted them to know.

We cleared a path to the village plaza, corralling women and children into lines on either side and turning them toward the center. We humiliated their men — spit on 'em, pistol whipped 'em, pinched their cheeks, treatin' 'em anything but human. Then, we fucking killed them, and we made their loved ones watch. I remember the way they looked. It was a hot day. The lands were dry, and the warm winds blew, kicking dust and caking villagers in desolation: old ladies, toothless and wailing to the heavens; children, dirty and cowering under their mothers' skirts; women with crying souls and desperate eyes.

We had already killed half their men. All the sun and murder was making us tired, and hell, we weren't getting the reaction we wanted. Sure, the villagers were hopeless, crestfallen: destroyed. But there were still too many defiant eyes. We had to put an end to it all.

So we put the little girl in the center.

She was the daughter of one of the rebels — we knew that much. We knew that she had brown skin, that she was a poor farmer, and that she was the enemy. And that's all we needed to know.

I was on crowd control. When the orders came through my radio, the executioners and their kneeling victims were far from where my combat boots left their imprints in the dust. My commander knew I didn't like killing like the others. So it surprised them, my willingness to kill the little girl. I just wanted to go home. I shut my radio off and start walkin' coolly down the path.

It's fuckin' hot. A crowd of dark eyes, bones, and rags surrounds me on either side. Heat, desperation, my own nerves: they make a heavy blanket and I wanna choke. But I keep walkin', focusing on my orders and suppressing all the rest. The crowd is weeping, soft and pathetic. Mothers hold their children close, wrapped under their rags. They want to feel like they can protect their babies, but they can't. Through the corner of my eye I see the iron mother, her children wrapped in her raggedy blanket, strong jaw still, wide nostrils flaring, dark eyes piercing my skin. She didn't cry at all, and that really bothered me. Later, when we dragged her screaming children away from her and she knew she was next, she wore the same face.

I keep walkin' past the shoeless, dirtcaked villagers — not lookin' at 'em but still taking it all in. A toothless grandmother falls to her knees on the side of the road, breaking my concentration. I glance down and see her tragic figure begging me for mercy in some language I don't understand. She's a desperate bitch and I spit in her direction.

I ignore the cold, empty stares of the motherless ragamuffins at the end of the row. I look to the center and see the rebel daughter on her bony knees, little arms tied tight behind her back.

I can see the color of her eyes across the killing field.

I grit my teeth and walk with more dedication toward her. I tell myself I have to kill her. I say it over and over in my head because I can't remember why. My brain screams out "they" — they're terrorists, they're communists, they're savages, they're brown. But to be honest, I don't really know who "they" are. Hell, I don't even know why we went to war, why we had to raze this village to the ground — and my whole life I spent wonderin' why I trudged the path, the reaper to a little girl. The best I can figure is because I was told.

I'm closing in now, and I can see the finer details of her face. Her eyes are beautiful and deep, and I wanna look away. I fix my gaze on what's left of the men behind her so I can rationalize what I'm doing, but I'm brought back to her eyes and I'm nearly paralyzed. It scares me, and the fear of losing control makes me angry. I reach for my holster and she doesn't flinch.

I draw my pistol and point it at the little girl's head, still a *few feet away. I bring it to her forehead and I can see all the details of the gun and my fingers wrapped around the trigger, the tendon of my forefinger running back along my flexing forearm, my arm hair running along and under the sleeves of the fatigues. I press the barrel hard into her skull. Her head tilts back slightly and her skin gives a little until I can feel the bone. I can see every little line of her face — the rich color of her beautiful blue-gray eyes and how her brown hair falls softly over them.*

Death is staring at her, and she's calm. I grit my teeth. I know she's stronger than me.

I'm about to pull the trigger when I hear a desperate voice cry out from the crowd. It makes me jump a little. It's her father. I start to think about how this makes me feel. I can see him rushing forward.

And then I blow her fucking brains out.

I watch the bullet's short journey through skin and bone and out the back of her head. Blood and bits of skull and tissue splatter all over me. She falls to my feet, and I drop my gun and look at my hands. There's blood all over them. I feel a suffocating heaviness, but then he comes up to me, placing his hand on my shoulder to reassure me.

"She had brown hair, and blue-gray eyes, just like my little Evee," I lament to the ground.

"Come on buddy," he soothes, "we got more killing to do."

My melancholy eyes meet his face.

Robert, the smiling good guy who says he understands but probably doesn't.

"They'll take care of us later..."

Robert, the guy who believes and follows the plan, the successful one who buys in.

"Come on, Walter. It's for the mission. It's the only way."

He stoops down and hands me my bloody gun, a comforting smile on his face like this all means something. I take it and try to believe, following him towards the center of the plaza where the last few men await execution.

After a few steps, something flashes in my periphery. Bare feet crunching dry dirt in the corner of my mind, I spin and point my gun. It's the little girl's father, running and yelling hysterically. He's saying something I can't understand right away, but later I'm pretty sure is "My little girl! They took my sweet little girl!"

I fire. He falls facedown in the dust. The kill comes with no remorse, and it's strange.

"Great shot, Walt!" Robert's congratulations float on the hot wind over my shoulder, "now you're gettin' it!" I stand still for a while, leaving his compliments unacknowledged in the stale breeze at my back. Then I turn around slowly, watching with dreamlike emptiness as he marches calmly toward the rebel men, his dirty boots stopping in front of their lowered eyes.

"You," he says, "are responsible for what's happened here today." He looks upon them with composed scorn, the weeping of women and children falling between his measured pauses. "You, the men who took up the fruitless cause of your leader, who deceived an entire village into betraying the greatest country on earth, the only country who has consistently shown you undeserving savages any generosity: you, yes you, you bandits...You took the helping hand of the United States of America, and you bit it, goddamnit!" Eyes still fixed on the men, he spits a long, heavy pool into the dirt. I can see the hate in his glare.

"So, before you die, just know that everything that happens here today...just know that all the atrocities will be in your name."

Robert stops. He looks into the horizon. Everything freezes in the wind.

...Then comes our commander's voice over the radio:

"Kill them."

Robert gives a slight nod and the executioners place their rifles at the back of the rebel heads. He grabs his radio.

"And the rest?"

Time stands still. We wait in the dust, hanging on the dying echo of his last question.

....Our commander's voice comes through the tinny speaker, rising eerily over the battlefield:

"This is war, son."

Robert nods softly, slowly turning the knob to shut off the radio. Before nightfall, all the villagers will be killed. By daybreak, all the villagers will be buried in one unmarked grave, and the world will never know.

....

It finishes. Nobody feels good, and we don't wanna look at each other. Even Robert has a doubtful look on his face as we dig, and later his eyes are painful and heavy. We can't grasp what we did, and we never will. We all just kinda stand there. We don't know what else to do.

Turns out, they have a plan for us. The higher-ups I mean. They know we're confused, scared. They know we're vulnerable.

But most importantly, they know what we know.

We'd really known it all along — we were just kidding ourselves until the massacre. After that, it was all pointless. We knew America had no principles, no regard for war conduct. We knew our country used people, and in just one night, countless transgressions culminated in mass murder and the destroyed lives and psyches of hundreds of heroic Americans — all for strategic gain in a hegemonic war with the rebels already on their dying leg. We knew it was all meaningless: bullshit. We knew what we had seen and what we had done.

And we weren't supposed to know a goddamn thing.

The horizon roars with wind chopped by three larger rescue planes. Dazed, unmoving, we look into the shimmering heat at our ticket back home. It's unusual for carriers to go unaccompanied by fighter jets — maybe the rebels weren't really that dangerous.

They divide us into three separate groups, give us pills to swallow for "dehydration," and corral us into the planes, each one going to one of three military hospitals located somewhere within the territory now controlled by the US. I can't remember much of the plane ride beyond the take-off, and I'm sure as hell blacked out by the landing. Guess that's what the pills are for.

There isn't much they can do for us there; or rather, there isn't much they can do to us. I eat lots of pills and watch American TV, and I listen to these recordings — strange medleys of spoken-word propaganda, patriotic tunes, and pop music. It plays over and over again in my mind. It's comforting, repetitive, numbing...

And then I wake up back stateside inside a dream inside a hospital, and we're all one general population, all the returning veterans bearing witness to the massacre. Most of our heads are so fucked up we can't say our own names, let alone recognize our platoon. Everything's so foggy, white...everyone so unknowingly familiar. I know we all share some horrible experience but I can't quite recall it, like a forgotten dream. But now as I sift through the fog, I can clearly remember Robert's face, unhappy and braindead as he sits in front of his drab food in the mess hall, bland smells and déjà vu churning my stomach. And the maniacal, coy smile of the young Dr. C burns deep in my retinas.

Dr. Calus is his real name. He devises this new program for returning vets. They call it revolutionary. Really, it's no more than a modern take on classical conditioning with heavy doses of drugs and shock therapy. His regimen is simple. Dr. Calus has us eat one of two drugs throughout any given day. One makes you loopy and the other makes you sicker n' hell. This second one's the kicker. It attacks the stomach via the brain: it's all psychosomatic. He gives it to us then asks us about our time in the war, shows us violent pictures, executions, beheadings, genocide, that sorta thing. By this time, the pills get it so our whole bodies are consumed by the tepid burn of the most skull numbing and gut wrenching nausea you can imagine. After a while, we develop a trained repulsion to the memory of the massacre as well as most of the war. Then more loopy pills and shocks to the brain to make us all forget, and repeat.

At first, I really trust them. I'm not sure how to deal with the pain, and it feels like they're helping. But now, I know it's all for them, it's all a ploy to erase my mind and history with it. One pill makes me hate a part of myself and the other one makes me wonder what parts are real. And as long as I

question whether or not the massacre happened, I can't do a
goddamn thing about it. Hell, most of my fellow veterans aren't
even that lucky. They never question what happened because
they know nothing did. You could say they were "cured."

After a while they arrange for us to be sent home for
ongoing therapy. Agents make regular house calls as "doctors"
to the patients involved in the massacre — they're check-ups to
see if the vets fall out of line. Most of them don't: they buy into
their diagnoses and pertinent therapies, forget about the war,
and move on with their lives as psychosis success stories.

I guess I don't go as quietly as the others. So I get the
"intensive treatment," the works: round the clock in-home
visits, a committed "daughter," group therapy, and
rehabilitation provided by the leader in military psychiatric
care. Slowly my regimen comes to define my sanity, control my
progress, to write my history. It robs me of redemption,
freedom — gnaws at my war crimes, making it so they never
happened, so I never happened. And the nameless atrocities
continue in all corners of the world.

Walter had one choice, and that was to kill them all.

XXIV

As October draws to a close in Northeast Indiana, the leaves take their final breaths, colors growing brighter until the early winter winds claim their lives. Spiders weave webs on fallen dead maples near building corners and porch stairs to stay warm. As autumn nights turn cold and clear, and the frost regularly visits the morning grass, spider webs become thicker, more intricate, and the stacks of crumbly leaves grow. But winter kills webs and leaves and weaves, no matter how pretty, and soon the spiders are forced to abandon their plot and move indoors, seeking the warm refuge of a sure death.

She was worried.

He was usually getting around at this time, preparing for their daily 7:30am walk. But on Wednesday October 24th, no sounds came from Walter's room.

At 7:24, she called the team.

By 7:26 they all sat in the living room, trading solemn looks.

She stood in the center, gnawing anxiously on the end of

her right thumb, her left arm folded across her body and nervously cupping her elbow. Her eyes were at the floor.

Dr. C cleared his throat. "Well, agent?"
She looked up.

"Subject has been sequestered in room all morning," she said matter-of-factly. "No typical morning din: no stirring, rustling, running water — subject is apparently abandoning Wednesday regimen."
"So, what do you propose?" he inquired.
"It's not quite 7:30, Dr. Calus," she remarked coolly. "He'll show for our morning walk."
Dr. C raised a quizzical brow.

"In 24 years, he's never missed it."

....

"Dad? Are you alright?"

She stood outside the heavy oaken door, her right hand against her rose-soft cheek, her left hand folded across her body to cup her elbow, a concerned look in her gentle face.

"Dad," she pleaded, "it's me, *your daughter*."

She waited patiently for sounds from Walter's

room — anything, even the soft friction of his whiskered face against the old bedroom carpet.

"Dad, please relax."

Silence.

A slow tear formed in her right eye, just below the blue-gray iris, rolling down, down, down her cheek like a melancholy whisper, gravity pulling it off her beautiful face and sending it free falling to the beige hallway carpet. The tear hit the floor with a soft thud, its heavy head folding in on itself only to expand back out again into a short lazy flood halfway absorbed by the carpet.

A second tear welled in her right eye, and a small sad pool slowly grew in her left. She sighed and let her head fall ever so slightly, a few strands of her glowing brown hair shielding her eyes, the rest tied back modestly in a shining brunette ponytail.

The second tear hit the carpet with a soft thud. It was all over.

Dad," she asserted despondently, "it's time for our morning walk."

Silence.

"Dad…" she began. She knew what she would say next. It was always two soft thuds and then the invitation for the morning walk. But if Walter remained silent for too long…

"…we're all we've got." The echo of her words died alone, and she knew something was wrong. She threw open the bedroom door.

Walter's room was empty.

His notepad lay open on the nightstand, turned to a hurried apology letter in his familiar scrawl:

"Sorry pumkin.
You were my favorite."

Her heart sank. She knew he was gone; she had known it all morning. *It's finally over,* she said to herself, closing the door gently. She smiled weakly at the long walls of family photos as she floated through the dim hallway and into the somber shadow of the living room.

Outside, Walter stood on a hill overlooking his house. He hadn't noticed it until this morning. He made his bed, donned his oversized jeans and patriotic cap, slipped into his faded gray jacket and crept into the early morning darkness of October 24th. Staying low to the ground, he found first one haunting black Impala, then another, planting Drain-o carbombs in tailpipes with cold, boney hands. He turned to go, and there it was — the hill, the climb: sweet, arduous, and beautiful. Now, atop the crown with long grass rustling at his feet and gentle breeze at his back, he had a great view. He was happy.

"....he knows," she said, her soft words hanging heavy in the room.

Robert and the others looked up with terror in their eyes. Dr. C leaned forward.

"How much?"

She could see the doctor trying to hide the fear in his face, and it disgusted her.

"All of it."

The house exploded in a flash of white light, shaking the neighborhood and leaving Walter's ear's ringing. He smiled, the heat from the inferno warming his face. He knew the Suits on patrol were rushing to their cars to check the scene; seconds later, Walter saw both Impalas burst into quiet, car-sized fireballs. He watched it all burn from atop the hill.

He stood still for a while, gazing into the flames and contemplating his new freedom. The late October breeze tickled his bones, telling him to get moving. November was coming. Soon, everything would be dead.

Walter turned and started walking, the heat on the back of his neck slowly fading. He didn't know where he was going, and he didn't really care.

Made in the USA
San Bernardino, CA
22 April 2016